Nomads

NewCon Press Novellas

Set 1: *(Cover art by Chris Moore)*
>The Iron Tactician – Alastair Reynolds
>At the Speed of Light – Simon Morden
>The Enclave – Anne Charnock
>The Memoirist – Neil Williamson

Set 2: *(Cover art by Vincent Sammy)*
>Sherlock Holmes: Case of the Bedevilled Poet – Simon Clark
>Cottingley – Alison Littlewood
>The Body in the Woods – Sarah Lotz
>The Wind – Jay Caselberg

Set 3: The Martian Quartet *(Cover art by Jim Burns)*
>The Martian Job – Jaine Fenn
>Sherlock Holmes: The Martian Simulacra – Eric Brown
>Phosphorous: A Winterstrike Story – Liz Williams
>The Greatest Story Ever Told – Una McCormack

Set 4: Strange Tales *(Cover art by Ben Baldwin)*
>Ghost Frequencies – Gary Gibson
>The Lake Boy – Adam Roberts
>Matryoshka – Ricardo Pinto
>The Land of Somewhere Safe – Hal Duncan

Set 5: The Alien Among Us *(Cover art by Peter Hollinghurst)*
>Morpho – Philip Palmer
>Nomads – Dave Hutchinson
>The Man Who Would be Kling – Adam Roberts
>Macsen Against the Jugger – Simon Morden

Nomads

Dave Hutchinson

NewCon Press
England

First published in the UK by NewCon Press
41 Wheatsheaf Road, Alconbury Weston, Cambs, PE28 4LF
January 2019

NCP 174 (limited edition hardback)
NCP 175 (softback)

10 9 8 7 6 5 4 3 2 1

ISBN:

978-1-912950-00-3 (hardback)
978-1-912950-02-7 (softback)

Cover art by Peter Hollinghurst
Cover layout by Ian Whates

Minor Editorial meddling by Ian Whates
Book layout by Storm Constantine

One

When we finally caught up with the Hinchcliffe twins it was gone two o'clock in the morning and they were doing seventy-five miles an hour in the direction of Huddersfield.

"Fair do's," Wally conceded, consulting the speed readout on the dashcam. "*I* wouldn't go down this road at much more than forty."

"That's because you're not a sociopath," I told him.

The brake lights of the Lexus ahead of us suddenly flashed red and disappeared into a dip in the road.

"Sharp right coming up," said Wally.

"Cheers." Three years and I still didn't know the roads as well as I should. I braked, took the corner at fifty, which was still way too fast. As we hit the straight again I could just see the Lexus' lights in the distance. "I'm never going to catch them, Wally."

"You don't have to," he told me. "Just be close enough to pull the daft little buggers out when they roll that thing."

"I'd let them burn."

He grunted. "Zero tolerance."

"Bloody right." I had to slow for another bend.

"I think you're gaining on them again."

I shook my head. The car I was driving could outrun and out-accelerate the car they were driving, but I was trying to keep my car on the road, and that made the difference; the twins literally didn't care.

The Hinchcliffes were a two-teenager crimewave, and it was a mystery to me why they weren't either in a young offenders' institution or dead by now. They could twoc any motor vehicle inside thirty seconds, they drove like people truly deranged, and if they didn't manage to smash up the vehicle they'd drive it until it ran out of petrol, strip it of any readily saleable parts, and torch it.

I'd been trying to catch them at it ever since I arrived in the village, but every time a car or van – or once, memorably, a bus – went missing and turned up as a bonfire forty miles away, the twins had an alibi. Granted, the alibis were usually provided by their mother, the legendarily fearsome Ursula, but I had never managed to find fault in any of them. That and the fact that we had never recovered any of the stolen property and nobody ever saw the little bastards commit the crime meant we could never hold them.

This time, though. This time...

"You know what they do in Florida?" Wally said mildly as I took a bump in the road a little too quickly and the car briefly became airborne.

"What." He was beginning to annoy me. My world had contracted to a narrow winding tunnel of hedges and dry-stone walls enclosing a strip of road illuminated by our headlights and the blue strobe on the roof, enlivened by the occasional glimpse of the stolen car's rear lights. It was like a video game. A really nasty, fast and terminally dangerous video game.

"They confiscate the possessions of criminals." Nothing much fazed Wally Mole, not even a high-speed pursuit along twisty roads at two in the morning. "Some of the police departments over there are hugely wealthy. They've got Porsches and executive jets and all sorts of stuff they've confiscated from drug dealers."

"Never work here." We hit another bend. This one was a bit tighter than it seemed, and I felt a muscle in my shoulder pop as I tried to steer into it. We bumped along the grass verge for a few metres before slewing back onto the road.

Wally didn't even seem to notice. "'spose not." He laughed. "What would we do with that old tractor Ursula's got outside her house?"

"I'm sure she'd suggest something." I caught sight of the Lexus's brake lights again; they seemed even further away.

Wally guffawed. "I'll bet."

The rear lights far ahead of us blinked in and out of existence as dips and humps and bends in the road hid and revealed them. It was becoming hypnotic.

"I think I've pulled my shoulder," I said.

He looked at me, a slim young Constable with sandy hair and a high-cheekboned face underlit by the screens of the radar and video and communications equipment installed in the dash. "You'd best stop then."

"Not a chance."

"You can't drive properly if you've hurt your shoulder."

"These sods have been the bane of my life ever since I got here. I'm not going to let them go this time."

"You'll get us killed. Pull over. I'll drive."

"Then *you'll* get us killed." Wally was widely known to be one of the worst drivers on the Force.

He said, "Frank —" and I saw the rear lights ahead of us do a remarkable thing. With incredible elegance, they tipped up on end and rose up on a fountain of sparks, turning lazily over and over around an eccentric axis that seemed to bear them into the sky.

"We have a stop," Wally gabbled into the radio. "We have a stop. They've rolled it. Four miles outside Stockford, on the Huddersfield road."

The lights of the Lexus were still cartwheeling across the night, jerking occasionally as the car hit something. It was an extraordinary thing to watch, and I almost rolled our own car watching it. I heard Colin Harvey over the radio, telling us that the emergency services had been dispatched to the scene and that other cars were on their way.

The road ran into a long shallow dip and then rose steeply along the face of a hillside. I slowed down as we reached the brow of the hill and the sharp bend at the top, and in the headlights we saw the tumbled hole in the near-side wall where the Lexus had gone out of control trying to get around the bend. I pulled the car up onto the verge and Wally jumped out, putting on his cap as he ran.

I sat where I was. It was suddenly very quiet. Wally must have switched off the two-tone as he got out. I felt as if I was still moving. I couldn't persuade my fingers to let go of the steering wheel.

"Frank." I turned my head. Wally was bending in through the open passenger door. "Come on."

That broke the spell. I opened my door and got out of the car, feeling wobbly-legged and not-quite-there, and followed Wally to the hole in the wall.

The wall ran along the very crest of the hillside. Looking over it, there was a sense of great open space below us, from which I could hear faint bleating noises. Far far away were little twinkling constellations of streetlights, and just below the horizon was a dull orange glow lighting the clouds that might have been Sheffield or Leeds or Huddersfield. I suddenly realised I had no idea where I was or which direction I was facing.

Closer to, down in the darkness, were two faint red lights. Wally had taken the lamp from the car, and shone it towards the lights, illuminating a great swath of grass dotted with panicking sheep running backwards and forwards and complaining at the top of their voices. Some sheep weren't moving, but lay in crushed mangled lumps, legs sticking out at peculiar angles.

The beam swept past an unusual object, came back.

"Fucking hell," Wally said.

The unusual object was the Lexus, and it was unusual because it was sitting on its side in a field on a hillside, leaking steam.

"Fiver they're dead," said Wally.

"You're on." I started to pick my way carefully down the hill. Wally followed a few steps behind and to my right, lighting the way. The air smelled of crushed grass and torn-up earth and sheep blood and petrol and exhaust fumes, and I thought I imagined music.

I heard Wally say, "Bollocks," calmly behind me, and the light swung wildly as he fell over. About a million candlepower flashed in my eyes as the spotlight bounced past me towards the wrecked car, and I was left blinking away peculiarly-coloured afterimages.

"Tripped over a sheep," Wally said.

"Nice one, Wally." I still couldn't see anything.

"Oh that's fucking disgusting," he said. "I just got these trousers back from the cleaners' as well."

My eyes were clearing slightly. I looked down the hill. The lamp had come to rest on a hummock of grass or a dead sheep or some other obstruction, shining more or less down on the crashed car. I blinked a couple of times and rubbed my eyes and went on down, collecting the lamp on the way.

The Lexus was lying on its right hand side. Its nearside wing was off in the darkness somewhere, as were the passenger door and the bonnet. The grass was scattered with glittering bits of glass, and looking back I could see great dark patches where the car had bounced and gouged chunks out of the hillside. I hadn't imagined the music; the car was still emitting a rhythmic thud-thud. Somewhere in the back of my mind, I was still watching those little lights wheeling over and over in the sky.

The whole car looked as if an over affectionate giant had hugged it. All four tyres were in shreds. I could hear sirens approaching on the road. I shone the lamp over the wreck, shaking my head. I'd wanted the twins, but I hadn't wanted them like this. This was dreadfully final.

"Bugger me," Wally murmured, finally reaching me, and for a few moments we forgot our job and just stood there looking at the mess the twins had made of the car.

Then there was a crackling grinding noise inside the Lexus and a head poked up out of the hole where the passenger-side door had been. The head looked around for a while, blinking away the blood that had run into its eyes. Finally, it saw us and gave us a ridiculous goofy grin.

"Howdo, Wally," said Graham. "Frank."

I turned to Wally. "You owe me a fiver," I said.

Two

As it turned out, neither Graham nor his brother, Barry, was seriously hurt. Cuts, bruises. Barry had a possible hairline fracture of the elbow. Wally went to hospital with them, partly to make sure they didn't try to steal the ambulance.

The capture of the Hinchcliffes was an event of such significance in the area that everyone wanted to claim to have been there. There were emergency vehicles parked all the way up the hill, a long line of flashing blue lights that was probably visible from orbit, and the wrecked Lexus was surrounded two-deep by paramedics and fire officers and police officers discussing the aftermath of the night's pursuit. From the number of vehicles, you'd have thought a major disaster had taken place here. Andy Housego, who did scenes-of-crime for half the police stations along the valley, was taking photographs. So were most of the crowd.

"I'll be able to sell these for a tenner a print," Andy told me, scrolling through the images on his camera's screen.

"Not if all these other people have their own," I said.

Andy obviously hadn't noticed anyone else taking pictures. He looked around and his expression changed. "Oi," he said, shooing some paramedics away from the car. "Bugger off. You'll contaminate the scene."

I smiled. About a hundred pairs of boots had tramped up and down the hillside tonight. Portable spotlights had been set up around the Lexus to illuminate it while firemen cut Barry Hinchcliffe out of the wreckage. The fire officers had their own video cameraman, a smug-looking bloke who I knew was thinking how much he could get for the tape from one of those television true-life disaster programmes. Andy was about two hours too late to worry about contamination of the scene. Not that it mattered terribly; the Hinchcliffes were going to be hard-pressed to find an alibi for this one.

On the way back up to the car, I noticed a little group of dead sheep. They had been arranged sitting up on a level area, leaning against each other, forelegs around each other's shoulders, like a bunch of old lads on a working-men's club outing to the seaside. I hoped somebody would have the presence of mind to dismantle this charming little tableau before a senior officer turned up or the Press arrived.

My radio made a sound like a llama gargling a handful of gravel. I pressed the transmit button and said, "Four-Oh-One."

More unintelligible noise.

"I can't understand a word you're saying, Colin," I said.

More unintelligible noise.

I sighed. "Give me a minute to get back to the car and I'll call you." Radio reception was notoriously spotty around here; Wally had had to call in his report from the car on the brow of the hill.

When I reached the car, I picked up the handset and said, "Four-Oh-One."

"Welcome back," said Colin.

"Have you any idea what you sounded like just then?"

"Like a llama gargling gravel. It's been commented on. What's your status?"

"Wally's gone to hospital with the twins and half the emergency services in the county are standing around the car taking photographs." I heard a strange noise in the background. "Control, is that *cheering* I can hear?"

"Don't let it go to your head, Four-Oh-One," Colin told me. "See if Dave's there and proceed to Dronfield Farm, off the Barnsley Road. Report of a prowler. Complainant is a Mrs Hallam."

I looked down the hill to the brightly-lit oasis of madness around the stolen car. "Control, can't someone else attend?"

"We can't spare anyone else."

"That's because everyone else is *here*, Control."

"You shouldn't even be there, Frank; you should have handed off and got yourself back here to make your report."

I checked my watch. Four o'clock. "Received." My shoulder started to throb.

Dave Beck was five or six years older than me and at least two stone heavier. He sat in the passenger seat like a badly-uniformed sack of coal, arms crossed, staring straight out through the windscreen.

"What's wrong?" I asked after five miles of annoyed silence.

Another couple of miles went by.

"You'll think you're clever now, then," Dave said without looking at me.

"Are you angry because you didn't get any photographs?"

Dave grunted and slumped deeper into his seat. He was born and bred in the area, had been in the Force much longer than me, and had begun his police career as a Constable toiling up and down between the little villages on an antiquated pushbike and giving road-safety lectures to infant school children. I was an incomer, I had never given a road-safety lecture in my life, and as far as I was concerned bicycles were part of the prehistory of the police force. And I had just made one of the most sought-after arrests in the area. Of course Dave hated me.

Dronfield Farm was a couple of miles outside the village. It was a long time since it had been a working farm; at some point in the early 1990s a businessman from Sheffield had bought it and entirely redeveloped the farm buildings into a luxury home. He'd wanted to build a couple of similar luxury homes on the rest of the land, but the Council had refused to give him planning permission, and when his business collapsed in the late '90s he buggered off, some said to the Costa del Sol.

The farm had changed hands a couple of times after that. There had been a millionaire rock star who had bought the place as a tax write-off and then moved in, claiming to be determined to return it to its original use, but all he left behind was a legacy of stories of drug busts and four-day parties. The last I'd heard it had been sold to a young couple from Leeds, who had been living there quietly and blamelessly for about a year and a half and therefore generating powerful local gossip about who they were and what they got up to.

My shoulder was really sore by the time I turned off the road and onto the short, narrow track leading to Dronfield Farm. As the stone walls drew in on us I flashed on a set of rear-lights somersaulting over and over and over in the darkness.

"My cousin used to farm here," Dave said.

"Pardon?" It was the first thing he'd said to me since accusing me of being clever.

"It was in the family for over a hundred years," he said.

That was all I needed: an already-annoyed Dave Beck returning to his family's dispossessed property. The headlights swept across a series of neat, new-looking buildings. As I pulled up in front of what seemed to be the main building the car set off an infra-red sensor and was suddenly pinned in a huge pool of blue-white light.

The door of the house opened as we were getting out of the car and putting on our caps. A tall young man wearing a dressing-gown over jeans and a teeshirt stepped out.

"What do you want?" he shouted.

It was hardly the worst reception I'd had since I joined the police service, but it was late and I was tired and my shoulder hurt and it was an effort to remain equable. "Mr Hallam?" I said.

He came over to the car. "What do you want? What are you doing here?"

I put on my best smile. "Are you Mr Hallam?"

"Of course I am." He was about twenty-five, tall and slim and good-looking, with tousled blond hair. Now he was close enough, I could smell alcohol on his breath.

"I'm Sergeant Grant. This is Sergeant Beck. You reported a prowler."

He stared at me. "No I didn't."

I managed to internalise a huge, world-weary sigh. It wasn't unusual for us to get prank calls. Most of the time it was kids, sometimes it was someone with a grudge against someone else, but you had to answer them all, just in case.

I said, "I'm afraid we received a call an hour or so ago reporting an intruder on your property, Mr Hallam."

His expression hardened. "Well, that wasn't –"

"It was me," called a voice from the direction of the house. "I called them."

We all looked over to the front door, where a figure was standing. Hallam said, "Oh, bloody hell, Leonie."

Dave and I exchanged glances. For the merest fraction of a

moment, we had both thought we could chalk this up to a prank call and go home.

"You take the statement," Dave said wearily, reaching into the car for one of the big torches. "I'll check the outbuildings."

"Right," I said. I turned to Hallam, who was shuffling uncomfortably from foot to foot, as if he needed to go to the lavatory. I looked down and saw that he was barefoot. It was quite a chilly night; the flagstones in front of the house must have been freezing. I said, "It's a bit nippy out, sir. Shall we go inside...?"

"I'll check the outbuildings," Dave said again.

"Yes, okay, Dave." I turned back to Hallam. "I'm sure it'll be the work of a couple of moments to sort this out, Mr Hallam, but shall we do it indoors before we all catch our deaths?"

He looked at me, at Dave, at me again, and I saw a look of anger cross his face so quickly that I almost thought I'd imagined it. Then he nodded and said, "Yes, this way."

The figure at the front door had gone by the time we reached it, and we stepped inside into a long, wide, flagstoned hallway with a ribbon of grey carpet running up the middle. About halfway along was a huge pair of glass doors, each with an oak tree etched on it. There were half a dozen white-oak doors along the white walls; one was half open and I peeked in as I went past and saw a large downstairs loo.

The hall ended in four wide, deep steps leading up to a space that seemed to have been fitted out like a consultant's waiting room with luxurious-looking black leather sofas arranged around a big green-marble-topped coffee table. In one wall a pair of french windows looked out onto darkness. To left and right, short corridors led off to other rooms.

"This is just a misunderstanding," Hallam said. "My wife's been a bit..."

"A bit what, sir?"

"Yes, Rob," said a voice I recognised from outside. "A bit what?"

I turned and saw a gorgeous young woman with the kind of strawberry-blonde ringlets that the pre-Raphaelites used to dream of. She was wearing jeans, an Oasis sweatshirt with mysterious multicoloured stains on the front, and a pair of Garfield slippers, and she was holding an immense chunky glass that contained about an inch and a half of an amber fluid I presumed was whisky. Her face was flushed and she seemed a little wobbly on her feet.

"Leonie," Hallam said to her. "What have you done, dragging the police out here at this time of night?"

She barely glanced at him. "Fuck off, Rob," she said. To me she said, "I don't know you, Constable."

"Sergeant Grant," I said, barely restraining the urge to touch the brim of my cap. "And you are...?"

"Yes." She took a big drink. "Yes, I am."

"This is Leonie, my wife," Hallam said. "We were..."

I looked around the living room. There was no sign of a fight – no overturned furniture or smashed crockery – but the Hallams' body language and general atmosphere in the room suggested that this was not, at the moment, a happy home.

I took out my notebook and said, "Perhaps you could tell me what happened, Mrs Hallam?"

She looked at me as if wondering where I'd come from all of a sudden. Then she seemed to remember. "Yes. I was working."

"Working...?"

She took another big drink. "I often work late, Constable." This time I didn't bother correcting her. "I illustrate children's books; I do a lot of my best work late at night." And she tipped her head over to one side as if daring me to disagree. Beside me, I could almost hear Hallam becoming more and more annoyed.

"What time was this?" I asked.

She shrugged. "Around two, I think. Maybe a little later. I heard something outside. I thought it was the wind rattling the outhouse doors at first." She turned and walked over to one of the doors and opened it. Looking through, I saw a cosy little beige-walled room full of flat-pack shelving and a single bed. In the middle of the room was a big draughting table and a high stool, and beside them a sort of cubical drawer-unit on castors with pens and bottles of ink strewn across its top. The lighting was arranged so that it mimicked daylight streaming through the windows, which didn't help the sense of unreality I was experiencing at the moment. There was a sheet of paper attached to the table, with a half-finished drawing of a tubby black cat talking to a jolly rosy-cheeked milkman. The milkman bore a disturbing resemblance to the local milkman, Alan Hall.

"I heard a noise outside," Mrs Hallam said again. "I got up and looked out of the window, but I couldn't see anything, so I thought it was the outhouse doors."

"Rattling in the wind," I said.

"Rob keeps saying he's going to fix them," she said, as if her husband wasn't in the same room with us. "But he never does."

"It's not windy tonight," I pointed out.

"It's *always* windy here," she told me. "Comes off of the fucking steppes and doesn't stop until it hits the Pennines. Would you like a drink?"

"No, thank you," I said. "Not while I'm on duty." I added, "And I'm driving the patrol car."

"Not from around here, are you," she said.

"Can we get back to the —"

"London?" she said. "I can hear London in your voice."

"I've lived in a lot of different places."

"But you've been here long enough to pick up an edge of accent." She beamed at me. "It's my hobby. Accents."

I blinked at her. Maybe I should have let Dave handle this.

Hallam sighed and said, "Leonie."

She barely glanced at him, but what glance there was told me everything I wanted to know about the state of the Hallams' marriage.

"I couldn't see anything outside with the lights on," she told me, cradling her glass in both hands. "So I turned them off." She looked into the study and her brow furrowed. "Then all of a sudden the security light went on and he was just standing in the courtyard."

"And?"

She shook her head, thinking. "He was just standing there, blinking. I think the light must have taken him completely by surprise because he was just... standing there."

"Can you remember what he looked like?" I asked. "How tall was he? Taller than me?"

She looked at me. "Don't patronise me, Sergeant. He was a little over six feet tall, quite well-built, with dark hair greying at the temples. He was wearing a light grey suit, a white shirt and a dark tie. He had dark shoes, probably black. He was about forty-five and fit-looking." Her lips twitched in a faint smile. "I have a pretty good memory too."

Well, there was nothing wrong with that. "And what did you do when you saw him?"

"I just stood there at the window. I don't think he saw me; he must have been blinded by the light. After a few moments he turned and ran away."

"All right." I took off my cap and scratched my head. The description didn't ring any bells.

"You're going to think I'm mad," she said.

I already thought she was a little out of touch with solid ground, but the drink might have done that. "Why?"

She took another sip of her whisky and seemed to be thinking about what she was going to say next. "I know him," she said finally.

Hallam looked at the ceiling in exasperation. "Good grief, Leonie," he said.

I could safely say that I had never had a night quite like this one. I said, "You know him, Mrs Hallam?"

All of a sudden she seemed unsure of herself. "Well, not *know*, exactly. I recognised him."

"Well that'll make our job a bit easier. Who was it?"

She looked straight at me and said, "It was Cary Grant."

"You were in there a long time," Dave said when I got back to the car.

"Something rum about the whole thing." Dave was sitting in the driver's seat so I went around and got in the passenger side. "I think they've been having a row."

"You think she made the whole thing up to get us out here?"

"Could be." I did up my seatbelt and looked at the house. "Nobody's hurt and there's no sign of a fight. I got the impression she's more likely to thump *him*. Did you find anything?"

He shook his head. "I could spit, the things they've done to this place."

"What about the prowler?"

Dave sighed. "Nah."

I looked out through the windscreen. The buildings of Dronfield Farm were beginning to come up out of the night as the sky lightened fractionally. Away in the distance I could just see the shapes of the hills against the sky.

"I'm off in an hour," Dave said, nodding at the dashboard clock.

"Back to base," I told him, settling back in my seat and suddenly feeling very very heavy. "And for Christ's sake drive carefully. I've had enough excitement for one night."

Three

By a combination of thrift and some small, unobtrusively lucrative investments, I had been able to afford to buy some land on the edge of the moors outside the village. It wasn't much, just a couple of acres of overgrown grassland that had once been part of a much larger farm. Ronnie Talbot, the estate agent, had walked me around it, waist-deep in grass, one drizzly Saturday morning with the clouds seeming to boil across the sky just above our heads, extolling its virtues and its possibilities.

Its virtues were a lovely view down into the valley on one side and what seemed like an infinite vista of moorland on the other, its relative inaccessibility with a single narrow winding track leading down to a barely-wider B-road that joined the Huddersfield road five miles outside the village, and the fact that it was very cheap because no one in their right mind would want to live here.

Its possibilities... Well.

"You have chosen to build your house in the worst place in fifty square kilometres," said Mr Keoshgerian. "Congratulations."

Mr Keoshgerian always told me something like this, so I just shrugged and tried to appear harmless.

"We are nowhere near connecting up the sewage and water services," he told me. "And we will not be unless you pay us another three thousand pounds."

I looked down at him. "I beg your pardon? How much?"

Mr Keoshgerian was an almost spherical little Armenian Cypriot who had come to West Yorkshire via a couple of decades in North

London. His accent would have provided Leonie Hallam with hours of innocent study.

"We have underestimated the amount of sewer-pipe we shall need to connect your house to the main sewer," he said, fiddling with his pipe.

I looked about me and said, "Well."

We were standing at the end of the narrow twisty track that led to what would one day be my home, God and Mister Keoshgerian willing. The immediate surroundings had changed since the day Ronnie Talbot first drove me up here in his tubercular little Simca.

The day after putting down the deposit on the land, I had come back in John Weller's Honda van and literally staked out the property, driving posts down at each corner and then stringing a couple of strands of wire between them, with smaller posts along the way to support them. It had taken me the whole of my day off and had been the best day's work I had ever done.

Now my land looked like a section of the Western Front dropped down onto the moors. My dream was a sea of churned mud and piles of brick and parked cement mixers, out of which a house was slowly rising.

The walls were up, the roof was on. There were no windows yet, and the floors were still rough unfinished concrete, but I could walk from room to room – I could even go upstairs, if I was careful – and imagine what it was going to be like when Mr Keoshgerian and his sons finally left.

It wasn't a big house, just five rooms on the ground floor and four upstairs. I had plans for one single huge room in the loft, but that could wait.

A strong gust of wind blew towards us across the moor. I could watch it coming, blowing the grass and heather, until it plucked Mr Keoshgerian's pork-pie hat off and bowled it across the ground. I watched him waddling off to catch it, thinking of Leonie Hallam talking about the wind last night. All the way from the steppes, and it doesn't stop until it hits the Pennines.

"And the gas and electricity," Mr Keoshgerian said, coming back to me with one hand clamped to the top of his head to stop his hat blowing off again. "Three thousand pounds. I have to hire a trenching machine."

"A what?"

"A trenching machine. Like a baby JCB. It will dig the trench for the sewer pipe."

"That's a lot of money for one trenching machine," I told him.

He gave a great shrug, a small, vivacious, olive-skinned man in his seventies dressed in Oxfam tweeds and a pair of green Wellingtons. "Mr Franks," he said around his pipe. "My son Kevin has a house which he would be more than willing to sell to you."

I laughed. Mr Keoshgerian had eight sons, all named after characters in the Bible, except Kevin, the youngest. He had been trying to sell me Kevin's house ever since we first met.

"It's a nice house," I said. "Kevin could get more for it than you're offering it to me for."

"Ah," he waved a hand. "Kevin hates his father. All he wants to do is move to London and go to rave parties."

Kevin didn't have to go to London for that, but I knew what he meant. I said, "We've already done a lot of work here, Mr Keoshgerian. It would be a shame to waste all that."

He bit down on the stem of his pipe and looked up at me. "I tell you what, Mr Franks." He tapped me on the chest. "We finish this house here, then we sell it to some fool from Sheffield for twice what it's worth and you buy my son Kevin's house. How's that?"

"It's an interesting plan," I admitted, and it was true. I could make a tidy profit on this place and Kevin's house was rather nice. It was just in the middle of the village, and I'd had enough of neighbours. There was another reason for my wanting to live here, but I didn't think Mr Keoshgerian would believe me, even if I felt inclined to tell him what it was.

Mr Keoshgerian said, "Ah," again and slapped my chest. "You policemen."

He always said that at some point, and I still had no idea what he meant by it. I looked around the building site. Four of Mr Keoshgerian's sons were working on the house, and eight of his employees. They'd built my dream precisely to my requirements, in all weathers, and I was going to miss them when the house was finished.

"This thing," I said.

"Trenching machine," said Mr Keoshgerian.

I was sure that wasn't its real name, but that didn't matter. "Try and negotiate the price down a little bit, Mr Keoshgerian. It sounds like something you should have considered when you tendered your estimate."

His entire face seemed to puff up around his pipe in indignation. "Are you accusing me of cheating you?" he demanded.

"No I'm not," I said. "But connection to the main services does seem rather a fundamental thing to have overlooked or underestimated, don't you think?"

He thought about it. He sucked on his pipe. He even took the pipe from between his lips momentarily, to show how serious he was, before returning it to his mouth.

"It seems to me," he said, screwing his eyes up against the wind, "that you want this place built bloody cheap."

"It's already twelve thousand over our original budget," I protested.

He nodded sagely. "And you have argued every penny with me."

"Not true," I said. "Every few hundred pounds, perhaps, but not every penny."

Mr Keoshgerian smiled. He loved his life and his work, and I had the feeling that setting obstacles up for me played a major part in his enjoyment. "It'll be right, Mr Franks," he said, reaching out and squeezing my bicep. He winked. "Just you worry about catching bad lads like the Hinchcliffes. Leave your house to me."

I scowled. "Word got around about that pretty bloody quickly," I said.

He beamed at me. "It's all over the village. You're a hero, Mr Franks."

Which was somewhere near the bottom of my list of things I wanted to be. "Wally Mole was there as well," I pointed out.

Mr Keoshgerian snorted. "Wally Mole."

"He's a good lad."

"He was at school with our Kevin. I could see he was stupid, even then."

"Wally is not stupid," I said. "He's a good copper."

Mr Keoshgerian sighed and shrugged. I was never going to convince him. On the other hand, he'd managed to make me forget all about the trenching machine.

On the way back into the village, I drove past Dronfield Farm and pulled into a lay-by a few hundred yards further down the road. I walked up the little lane to the gate and leaned on it, looking up the gravelled driveway into what had once been the farmyard. The buildings had been cleaned up, the stone sandblasted and new windows installed. It didn't look very much like a farm any more.

While I stood there, Leonie Hallam emerged from around one of the buildings, saw me, and walked down the driveway to the gate.

"I almost didn't recognise you out of uniform, Sergeant..." she said.

"Grant," I said.

"Yes," she said. "Can I help you?" She was wearing a green waxed jacket and jeans, and there were green Wellingtons on her feet. Her face was scrubbed and her hair was tied back. She looked a lot younger than I remembered.

"I was just passing," I told her. "I thought I'd look in and check you hadn't had any more trouble."

She shook her head. "Nothing I've noticed. Have you caught him?"

"I'm afraid not. Not yet."

She tilted her head to one side and looked at me. "And here was me thinking you'd come to bring me some good news."

"You seemed a bit upset the other night," I said.

"I'm not surprised; I'd just seen a strange bloke wandering around outside."

"Was that all it was?"

She narrowed her eyes at me. "Isn't that enough, Sergeant?"

I decided to let it go. "We're going to be stopping by, from time to time," I told her. "Just to make sure you don't have any more unwelcome visitors. And my Inspector's arranging a visit from someone who can advise you on home security."

"I don't think that's necessary," she said. "The place was already like a fortress when we moved in."

Courtesy, no doubt, of the rock star who had once lived here. I said, "It won't hurt to have someone check. And it's free." She kept looking at me. "But it's up to you. Free country and all that."

"I'll talk it over with my husband," she said. "Anyway, it's been nice to see you, and thank you for taking the trouble to stop by, but I have to get back to work."

"Of course. Mustn't keep you. If you do have any more trouble, though, call us immediately. I'd like to find this chap, if possible."

"You think he might be dangerous?"

"Maybe not, but most of the farmers round here keep shotguns; I'd like to sort this out before someone gets hurt." When she didn't reply I nodded and said, "Anyway, have a good day, Mrs Hallam."

"Yes," she said, and she turned and walked back up the drive.

I watched her go for a few seconds, wondering what I'd done to offend her. Then I headed for my car.

Like a lot of villages on the old coach-roads, Stockford had grown up around its coaching inn. It hadn't grown up very much, though. There were two steep streets of houses and little shops running down towards the valley bottom, a scatter of outlying farms, a Forestry Commission plantation, and a dozen or so light-industrial units. In the normal course of events, its police station would have been closed years ago and the responsibility for policing the area would have devolved to a station in one of the larger villages closer to Barnsley or Huddersfield, but some bureaucratic brainstorm had occurred at Force HQ and we not only had a police station but twelve officers and four patrol cars as well. John Weller, my Inspector, said he spent at least five minutes every day worrying that HQ would notice that we were still here and decide we were costing them too much money.

Because my house wasn't yet fit for human habitation, I was living over the shop, in one of the bachelor flats above the police station. It was bright and airy and had all the amenities, but no matter how much air freshener I sprayed about it always smelled faintly of disinfectant, and on Saturday nights you could always hear some drunk or other shouting in the cells.

It was also difficult to get away from the Job.

I was cooking dinner when there was a knock on the front door. "It's open!" I shouted rather than answering the door, because my hands were covered with a mixture of flour and egg.

The door opened and John looked into the flat. "You're busy," he said.

"Just having a bite to eat. Come on in."

He came in and closed the door behind him. "What are you cooking?"

"Pork escalope, duchesse potatoes and mange touts."

He shook his head. John remained indelibly imprinted with the solid meat-and-two-veg ethos that he had learned from his mother's cooking. To him, a square meal was one that came with lashings of Oxo gravy. My menus might as well have been written in a foreign language.

I held up the meat. "You get a nice lean cut of pork, and you beat it flat with a hammer." I held up the meat hammer in the other hand. "This tenderises the meat. Then you dip it in flour, then in beaten egg, then –"

He held up a hand. "All right, Frank."

"It's really easy, John," I told him. "You can do it with chicken breasts as well. Turkey breasts. *Veal.* Yum yum." I smacked my lips.

"Frank."

"All you need is a bit of meat, a couple of eggs, some flour and some breadcrumbs and a bit of seasoning, and it's really nice. I'll teach you. Go home tonight and surprise Lucy."

He looked levelly at me. I sighed and put the pork on a plate and the meat-hammer on the worktop. "I can't believe in this day and age that you've never learned to cook for yourself." I turned off the gas under the frying pan, turned to the sink and rinsed my hands under the tap.

"I haven't had a chance to say well done for arresting the Hinchcliffes," he said, short-circuiting the conversation about his culinary shortcomings.

"Wally was there too," I pointed out, drying my hands on a towel.

"You were driving the car."

"Wally wanted to."

He smiled. "If he had done I'd have been visiting you in hospital."

"Doesn't matter. He was there." I went through into the living room, sat down on the sofa and started to roll myself a cigarette.

"I've read your report," he said, following me and flopping into one of the threadbare armchairs.

"And?"

"Oh, brilliant, as usual. Every full stop and comma in the right place. Semi-colons. Ah." He looked at the ceiling and smiled nostalgically. "I thought I'd never see another semi-colon again after I left college." He caught me looking cynically at him. "No, I mean it. Some of these lads can hardly put two words together on a page. Your reports are a joy to read. Can I tell you a secret?"

"You can give it a try."

He sat forward on the chair and clasped his hands together between his knees. "Sometimes," he said seriously, "I take your reports home and read them before I go to bed, just so I can go to sleep knowing the force isn't entirely in the hands of illiterates."

I smiled at him. "Fuck off, John."

He shrugged and sat back. He was only five or six years older than me, and he was starting to get fat. He was still wearing his uniform trousers and shirt, but he'd removed his clip-on tie and undone the top button of his shirt and his thinning brown hair was a little tousled.

"And in all those pages of gorgeous prose, I detected a definite reluctance on your part to take any credit for what you did the other night," he told me.

"Oh, John," I said.

"We've been trying to put the Hinchcliffes away ever since they were old enough to go in the newsagents' and steal copies of *The Dandy*," said John. "We know they've been involved in at least forty percent of all the crimes committed in this area over the last eight years, and we've never been able to charge them for any of them."

I rubbed my eyes.

"This goes no further than you and me, right?"

I nodded.

"Some of the lads were talking about going up to Hinchcliffe Farm with baseball bats and sorting out the problem."

I stared at him.

John nodded. "Well, it never came to that, did it."

I didn't know what to say. I was trying to reassess my relationship with my fellow officers. It hadn't realised I was working with people who had vigilante tendencies.

"You'll take credit for this collar, Frank," John told me. "And that's an order."

"You can't give me an order; you're not wearing your tie." I licked the sticky-strip on my Rizla and rolled my cigarette shut. Then I started to search through the pile of newspapers and magazines on the coffee-table for a bit of card to use as a filter.

"I can't understand you," he said. "The most significant arrest in this area since..." He thought about it "...well, *ever*, and you don't want to take credit for it."

I scowled and tore a strip off the cover of a copy of *New Scientist*. "As I understand it, we don't do this job for brownie points."

"There's brownie points and brownie points. You understand what I mean?"

"No, John. I don't." I rolled up the strip of paper and inserted it in the end of my cigarette. Then I put the cigarette in my mouth and lit it. A shower of burning tobacco sifted down onto my lap. I was the world's most inept roll-your-own smoker, but I knew that if I bought ready-mades I could quite happily notch up three packets a day. By rolling my own I at least managed to limit the amount of tobacco I smoked; a high percentage of it just fell out. I patted my jeans to put out the tiny little cinders.

John said. "Ursula's made a formal complaint against you."

"Well, that's hardly new."

"She says you wilfully endangered the twins because you have a personal grudge against them."

I stared at him.

"Oh, it'll never fly, of course," he said. "The car was nicked, we've got your dashcam footage, and even the twins won't be able to deny they were there. Ursula's saying you panicked them into driving like that, though."

"It's a novel idea," I said, "considering they were already doing seventy-five when Wally and I first sighted them."

"Like I say, we've got your footage of the pursuit. It won't stand up, but you should be aware that the IOPC will be in touch about it."

I sighed. The Independent Office for Police Conduct were exactly what I needed in my life right now.

"There'll be someone over from Sheffield to interview you in a day or so," he told me. "Just stay calm and tell them the truth and everything will be fine." He watched my face for a few moments. "You've dealt with the IOPC before."

"Once."

"They're all right, really," he said. "Just doing their job. They hate being lied to, though. So keep it on the straight and narrow. Your report's fine; stick to that."

"We didn't really follow procedure out there," I reminded him. "After the twins rolled the car."

He scowled. He'd seen some of the photos of the little carnival which had gone on at the crash site, and he knew as well as I did that we were one social media posting away from a public relations catastrophe. It was only a matter of time. "Let's deal with one disaster at once, Frank," he said. "You're on administrative leave until the IOPC have had a chance to interview you. I would tell you not to contact any of the officers involved with the incident, but you live in the police station so just try to stay out of everyone's way. Do *not* try to contact Ursula Hinchcliffe." As if I would ever do that under any circumstances.

I said, "This is very annoying, John."

"I know. But it's just routine. Tell them what happened, tell them the truth, and it'll all be over in a few days."

I stubbed out my cigarette. "Okay."

He got up and went to the door. "Oh, I got a call from Leonie Hallam."

"Has she made a complaint as well?"

"She was wondering what you were doing out there this afternoon."

"I'd been up to the house, it was on the way back," I told him. I shrugged. "I just thought I'd look in."

He watched me for a few moments. "What did you talk about?"

"I asked her if she'd seen anything else out of the ordinary since I was last there, told her we were going to run extra patrols past the farm, mentioned sending someone to check their locks and alarms. She seemed a bit annoyed with me being there, so I left. I didn't go onto the property; we talked at the gate."

"Hm." John put his hand on the door handle. "You said in your report that you thought there might be a domestic situation there."

"It was just a feeling; I got the impression she and her husband had been rowing. They'd both been drinking – she was still drinking while I was there – but I didn't see any signs of a fight."

"Okay." He turned the handle. "Let me have a think about that. But do me a favour and don't go out there again without letting me know."

"Sure," I said. "Not a problem."

"And don't worry about the IOPC. Everything will be fine."

"Yes," I said. "Yes, I'm sure it will."

Four

A couple of days later, I was called down to the interview room, and found a couple already sitting there. She was middle-aged and untidy; he was younger and smartly-suited. There were official-looking folders on the table in front of them.

"Sergeant Grant," the woman said, standing as I walked in. "Rhona Sachs." She put out her hand and I shook it. "This is my colleague, Colin Richmond," she added, indicating the younger man, who hadn't bothered to stand and didn't offer to shake my hand. "May I call you Frank?" she asked, sitting again.

"By all means," I said, sitting down opposite them.

"I understand you've waived your right to be accompanied by a Police Federation rep," she told me, putting a voice recorder on the table and switching it on.

I put my phone down beside the recorder and turned on the voice memo app. "Let's not bother the Fed until we have to," I said.

She nodded. "So," she said. "We're here because a complaint has been brought against you by a Mrs Ursula Hinchcliffe. Do you know Mrs Hinchcliffe?"

"Only by reputation. We've never met." I watched Richmond note this down on a clean sheet of paper.

"Right." Sachs smiled at me and clasped her hands on the table. "Well, this is all perfectly routine and we'll try to make it as painless for everybody as possible."

"Painless is good," I said.

She smiled again. "Indeed. So, to start with, why don't you tell us what happened on the evening of the seventeenth? In your own words."

I took them through what had happened, from receiving the call to be on the lookout for a stolen Lexus, to spotting the car being driven at high speed, setting off in pursuit, the Lexus crashing. I was more vague about the aftermath, with everyone taking photographs. Sachs asked questions when she thought a point needed clarifying. Richmond remained silent, taking notes.

When I'd completed my account, Sachs said, "Mrs Hinchcliffe alleges that the officers at this station were engaged in a vendetta against her sons. Would you say that's a fair comment on the situation?"

"I wouldn't say it was a *vendetta*," I said.

She sat back and watched me. "What would you say it was then, Frank?"

"The twins are responsible for quite a high proportion of the crime around here," I told her. "We've been keen to arrest them for some time."

She nodded. "*Keen.* By any means necessary?"

"No, of course not. The longer they're put away the longer things will be quiet round here; nobody would want to jeopardise that."

Sachs looked at me a moment longer, then she opened one of the folders and consulted some notes. "And then you were despatched to… Dronfield Farm," she said, reading. "A reported intruder. Shouldn't you have come straight back here and written up your report about the accident?"

"It was a busy night. Dronfield Farm was on the way back here. Control thought I could kill two birds with one stone, stop off and deal with the prowler report and then carry on back to the station."

"And that's what happened?"

"Yes. I took statements from the householders, Sergeant Beck checked the property. There was no sign of an intruder."

"How long were you at Dronfield Farm?"

"About thirty minutes."

"That doesn't seem very long," she said. "To take two statements and do a check of the property."

"The householder who reported the prowler had been drinking. I got the impression that she and her husband had been having a row. I made a judgement not to expend time and resources on it

29

unnecessarily. And, as you said, I should have been back here making my report."

"Cary Grant," said Richmond. They were the first words he had spoken since I arrived in the room. I looked at him. He'd stopped taking notes and was watching me. "Mrs Hallam said the intruder was Cary Grant."

"Those were her words, yes."

"Not 'he *looked* like Cary Grant'."

"As I said, she'd been drinking. Was still drinking."

Richmond made a note. Sachs said, "Why would she say that?"

"It happens more often than you'd think. People are familiar with the faces of famous people; sometimes they just subconsciously associate them with people they've seen. We had a distraction burglar about eighteen months ago, two of the victims said he looked like George Clooney."

"Did he?" asked Richmond.

"I don't know. We haven't caught him yet."

Richmond looked at me a few moments longer, then made another note.

"And what happened after that?" Sachs asked.

"As I said, Sergeant Beck checked the property while I was taking statements. I issued the Hallams with a crime number, and we left."

"And Sergeant Beck found no sign of an intruder?" she said.

"That's right."

"Were there any other intruder reports that night?" asked Richmond.

We seemed to have drifted quite a distance from the purpose of this interview. "There were a couple. We get at least one, most nights."

"Did you see anyone else at Dronfield Farm?" Sachs asked. "Maybe had an impression that someone else was in the house?"

"I'm afraid I don't follow."

She smiled. "We're just trying to get a sense of your state of mind that night. It must have felt quite strange to go from a high-speed chase to something as mundane as a prowler report."

Thinking of Leonie Hallam's call to the station, I said, "Have the Hallams made a complaint as well?"

"No," she said. "No, they haven't. Is there any reason why they should?"

"Not so far as I can recall, but presumably I was so traumatised by the pursuit that I wasn't able to do my job properly."

Richmond put down his pen again and looked at me. Sachs looked sad. "No one is suggesting that you weren't, Frank."

I started to wonder whether it had been a good idea not to have a Fed rep in the room with me. "So what *is* the suggestion here, Ms Sachs?" When neither of them answered, I stood up. "I'm done."

"We'll tell you when you're done, Sergeant Grant," Richmond told me. "Sit down."

"Frank," Sachs said in a gently chiding tone of voice. "Don't be so dramatic."

I stayed where I was.

"This is all completely routine," Sachs explained patiently. "We're required to investigate when a complaint is made."

It was not remotely routine. I'd had a run-in with the IOPC a couple of years ago, when a drunk driver I'd arrested made a complaint that I had damaged his car. That had involved me sitting down with someone for half an hour and going through my report, not trying to establish my state of mind in the hours after the arrest.

I said, "I'd like to speak to my Fed rep."

"Oh, Frank," said Sachs, sitting back in her chair and crossing her arms. "You were doing so well, too. Coming here voluntarily, unrepresented, as if you're completely innocent."

"I *am* completely innocent."

She wrinkled her nose at me. "Come on," she said. "Nobody's *completely* innocent."

Richmond opened one of his folders, took out an A4-sized printed photo, and held it up so I could see it. The quality was grainy, but there was no problem making out the little group of dead sheep propped upright on the hillside, front legs round each others' shoulders. You had to work a little harder to identify figures in the background, but there I was, captured at a moment where I looked utterly clueless, which to be fair wasn't hard to do. Richmond gave me a few more seconds to consider the scene, then he put the photo away again.

"We're keeping a lid on this for the moment," Sachs told me. "But we still haven't identified everyone who was at the scene. There's no telling when this will leak."

"*We?*"

Richmond pushed a pen and a blank sheet of paper across the table towards me. "If you could give us a list of everyone you remember seeing there, it would be helpful," he said.

"I already did that in my report," I told him.

"Well it'll be easier to do it again then, won't it," said Sachs.

I stood looking at them, weighing up possibilities. Richmond and Sachs were not from the IOPC, and this interview was not about Ursula Hinchcliffe's complaint. I knew that, and they knew I knew it, and how I reacted in the next few minutes was going to tell them whether their suspicions about me – and surely they could only be suspicions, unless someone had leaked in a catastrophic way – were correct or not.

I nodded at the pile of folders on the table. "That circus was nothing to do with me," I said. "And before you tell me I should have stopped it, you should have been there."

Sachs was watching me with a little smile on her face. She said, "You didn't mention anything about it in your report. Just 'ensured the scene was secure, then responded to a report of an intruder at Dronfield Farm'."

"The scene *was* secure," I said. For an hour or so, it had probably been the most secure place in the county. It had certainly had the highest density of police officers. I sat down again and picked up the pen. "I'll never be able to remember everyone who was there."

"Just do your best," Richmond told me. "There's a good chap."

Afterward, I went back up to the flat and stood for a while at the window, looking down on the High Street. Presently, Richmond and Sachs's car emerged from the yard behind the police station, paused for a moment, then turned in the direction of Sheffield and drove off. I scratched my head and wondered what they knew, what they thought they knew. They couldn't possibly know everything; their body language would have been entirely different. They'd been relaxed, in control, and I couldn't imagine anyone being able to pull that off if they knew the truth.

They knew something, though. That business about Dronfield Farm was suggestive. So, what did they have? A rumour? A hint? Something in the breeze?

I had a plan for this eventuality, of course, caches of identities scattered around the country and here and there in Europe. I'd never seriously thought I would need them, but it had seemed rational to have the option. Down the years I'd thought about it less and less, and I wondered if that was a symptom of me getting comfortable, getting sloppy.

On the other hand, if they did think they knew something, they – whoever they were – would be waiting for me to bolt. Until I knew what this was about, until I got a handle on whether I could ride it out or not, it might be best to carry on as normal.

Sod it. I went and cooked myself dinner.

Five

Nothing much happened for the next couple of days. John informed me that pending the IOPC's report I was still on administrative leave. I thought we might be waiting a while for any 'report', but I didn't share my suspicions about Sachs and Richmond. I spent most of my time up at the house, helping Mr Keoshgerian's sons cable the place before the plasterers moved in. It was work I could do almost literally with my brain in neutral, and it helped take my mind off what was going on elsewhere in my life, although I couldn't help the nagging feeling that it was all for nothing, that I was going to have to leave it all behind.

Every day, driving home, I passed Dronfield Farm. There was no choice really – any other route would have taken me five or ten miles out of my way – but I had a feeling that I would have been doing it anyway. Most of the time, the farm seemed deserted, but once I saw a figure standing in the lane. It could have been Leonie Hallam, it could have been her husband. It could, for all the brief glance I had of it as I went by, have been Cary Grant.

Evenings, I cooked, read, took care of paperwork that had been building up. Late at night, I did some discreet research online. I sat at the window and looked down on the High Street. Apart from the Black Bull at the other end, and a couple of takeaways, the street pretty much shut down around eight in the evening. By midnight it was completely deserted, save for the occasional car. I liked it here, and I liked being a police officer. It was a quiet, simple life, and now it was becoming complicated again and I needed to know why before I could decide what to do about it.

The police station had been built in the mid-1930s, a faintly grim three-story piece of West Yorkshire civic architecture rendered in local gritstone. It could have been a smallish town hall, if you ignored the blue lamp hanging over the front door and the big glass-fronted noticeboard in which various ancient posters were bleaching slowly in the occasional sunshine. Its walls were thick, its floors covered with lino, and its central heating charmingly outdated. The most modern thing about it was the enormous transmitter mast in the yard at the back, which carried our comms and formed part of the civil defence network,

There were three flats on the third floor, but only mine was occupied. The only ways to reach it were either past the front desk and then through two security doors and up the stairs, or via the rickety fire escape attached to the end of the building. It made getting in and out without being seen tricky, but I'd long ago spoofed the alarm on the door which led to the fire escape, and the building's security cameras had belonged to me since not long after I'd moved in. I checked them quickly on my laptop just after midnight, clicking from one view to the next. Everything seemed quiet; most of the shift was out on patrol, the cells in the basement were empty, the canteen was closed, the duty sergeant at the front desk looked as if she was tackling the local newspaper's crossword. I typed a couple of commands which captured a few seconds' footage from the cameras on the third floor and outside and played it back into the system on a loop, then I got up and quietly and unhurriedly left the flat.

The door to the fire escape was at the end of a short corridor. I unlocked it, stepped out onto the platform beyond, locked it behind me. I stood for a few seconds, looking and listening. Nobody about, no vehicle engines. I walked quickly down the metal stairway, then climbed over the fence which surrounded it at the bottom. Another moment to look and listen, and then I was walking away from the police station.

I habitually parked my car down a side street a hundred yards or so from the station, partly because the secure compound was too small for all our vehicles and there was never any space, but mostly so I could do what I was doing now without having to go through the noisy and noticeable palaver of opening the gates. Five minutes after closing the door of my flat, I was on the road and no one knew I was gone. No one was going to come visiting the flat at this time of night – I barely had any visitors as it was – and I was on leave, anyway. Short of a complete breakdown of civil order and the need to call out every available warm body, nobody would miss me.

Ten minutes out of the village on the Barnsley road, I passed Dronfield Farm. I didn't slow down. About half a mile further on, I came to a junction where a twisty forestry road met the main road. I turned onto it and drove slowly until I came to one of the Forestry Commission plantations dotted about the area, and I parked. The chances of anyone being out here at this time of night were vanishingly small, and I was hidden from the main road. I got out, locked the car, and set out to walk through the forest.

It wasn't, to be honest, much of a forest. You could walk across it from edge to edge in less than twenty minutes, and I soon reached the edge of the trees and found myself looking out across a field at the boundary of the Hallams' property.

By the standards of the natives, my night vision was abnormally good. I hung back just inside the wood and walked along until I reached the corner nearest Dronfield Farm. The place looked deserted; the house and its outbuildings were in darkness and I couldn't see any vehicles. Keeping the wood behind me, I walked straight out across the field until I reached the fence around the farm.

It wasn't much of a fence, just four strands of wire strung between a line of posts. Long grass grew up against it, where the owner of the field hadn't bothered to cut up to the edges. The wire was old, patinated, the posts moss-stained concrete. No obvious countermeasures. I walked along the fence until I was hidden from view of the main house by one of the outbuildings. Here, the long grass was trodden down a little, as if a fox or something larger had come this way a few days before. I looked around on the ground, but there were no signs that a person had been here, no discarded cigarette ends or sweet wrappers or empty soft drink cans.

Thus far, I had not really done anything wrong. I'd gone for a midnight drive because I couldn't sleep, and I'd stopped and got out to stretch my legs, and my word, was I really *that* close to Dronfield Farm, Inspector Weller? John might frown at me, if he ever found out I'd been here, and it would colour our working relationship, quite possibly permanently, but really there was nothing he could do about it.

What I did next, though, felt a lot like stepping off the top of a tall building, that moment when gravity takes over and there is absolutely no way to go back. Crouching down, I slipped between two of the strands of wire and onto Dronfield Farm.

On the other side of the fence, I stood very still, listening. Apart from the ever-present sigh of the wind blowing across the moors, the world seemed completely silent. No cars on the road, no animals moving in the undergrowth, no sounds from the buildings of Dronfield Farm. It was as if I was the only person on earth. I wasn't sure whether that was a good or bad thing.

I walked up to the back of the outbuilding and peeked around the corner at the main house. There was no sign that anyone was home. Staying out of range of the intruder light sensors, I moved round until I could get a good look at the yard. It was laid with gravel that showed the marks of vehicles, and the outbuildings that had once contained various bits of agricultural equipment and general farm stuff had been repaired and cleaned up. One large newer outbuilding was fronted with two large doors with little round portholes in them at head-height. I peeked through one of them; it seemed to be kitted out as a garage, although there was no car inside. Ditto for the next one.

I walked around the perimeter of the property, staying just inside the fence. At the back of the main house there was a little formal garden, surrounded by a waist-high wall. A pair of french windows that I remembered from my visit a few nights ago looked out into the garden. Beyond the doors, the lounge was dark and deserted. I stood there looking at them for quite a while. A car passed, out on the road, one of our patrol vehicles making a visit, judging by the sound of the engine. It barely slowed as it passed, which was sloppy. I stood where I was until it had disappeared into the distance.

Out here beyond the edge of the village, the presence of an intruder suggested either burglary or violence. Back in Stockford, you got drunks wandering into peoples' gardens or getting confused and trying to open the wrong door, or opportunity theft when some toerag spotted an open window or an unlocked door. But here, out on the moors, it signified real intent. Pretty much all the farms in the area had had something stolen down the years, whether it was livestock or bits and pieces of agricultural equipment or actual vehicles. A couple of years ago we'd had a crew of lads from Coventry who came up here nicking tractors and quadbikes to order from outlying farms. They were pretty efficient, but one night, returning down the M1 after a successful raid, their truck jacknifed and crashed through the central reservation, causing a twenty-vehicle pileup and killing themselves and thirty-seven others, and that was the end of that.

One theory was that the intruder at Dronfield Farm was the advance man for a gang which had been looking for new targets using maps to identify properties labelled 'farm'. When it became obvious that it wasn't a working farm any more, the theory went, the gang would have moved on, but by now we knew they were in the area. John Weller had circulated an advisory to all the outlying farms and properties, asking people to keep their eyes open for strangers, but there had been no reports so far, and I doubted there would be, because there was no gang. There was only Cary Grant, and that was a problem I couldn't share with anyone.

There had been closed-circuit cameras at the farm, installed by a previous owner, but the Hallams had told Andy Newman, our security expert, that the system had malfunctioned not long after they moved in and they hadn't got round to repairing it. Andy had wagged a finger at them and tut-tutted, but he'd told me that Leonie and her husband hadn't seemed particularly bothered. He'd got the impression that the most important thing for them was to let him finish his security assessment and then leave as soon as possible. John Weller thought this was another indicator of some sort of domestic violence situation at Dronfield Farm, but I suspected there was a wholly different explanation.

There was no point in going any further onto the property. If I was right, in the absence of cameras, there would be other, less obvious, countermeasures and I didn't want to tangle with those. I walked back to where I'd crossed the fence and stepped back into the field.

I was halfway back to the car when I heard the sound of rapid footsteps in the short grass behind me. I just had time to half-turn and see a figure rushing towards me, and yes, it was Cary Grant.

The pain woke me, and it was so severe that I almost passed out again. My head and chest were in agony; every time I took a shallow breath there was a razoring of broken ribs. My left leg felt broken, and peering down at my left hand I saw it was useless, crushed, the fingers sticking out at odd angles. There was blood in my mouth.

I must have made a sound because Wally said, "Frank?"

I slowly, agonisingly, turned my head and looked at him. We were in his car and he was hunched over the wheel, concentrating on the road. "Why are we in your car, Wally?" I asked. Then I had to say it again because my mouth was swollen and the words came out mushy and malformed.

"Jesus, Frank," he said. "What happened to you? What were you doing out there at this time of night?"

"Why are we in your car?" I asked again.

"You phoned me, don't you remember?"

It was hard, just then, to remember my own name. I kept catching myself on the edge of drifting back into unconsciousness. "Where are we going?"

"A&E," he said.

"No," I said. "No, no. No hospital."

"Don't be stupid," he said. "Look at the state of you. Who did this?"

"No hospital," I said again. "Take me home."

"We've only got first aid at the station, Frank. You need a hospital."

I tried to shake my head but the pain was just too great. "Not the station," I said. "Home. My house."

That was a mistake, because the surprise almost made Wally lose control of the car. "What?" he said when he was back on the right side of the road. "Why?"

"Take me to the house," I said as calmly as I could. "It's important. Life or death." I had no idea if this was true or not. It certainly felt as if it was.

"No," he said, shaking his head. "No way."

"Wally, seriously, that's an order."

"No," he said again. "I'm taking you to hospital."

I sighed and almost blacked out from the pain in my chest. Punctured lung? I would probably be dead by the time Wally got me to the nearest Accident & Emergency department. I said, "Okay, Wally, you win. Stop off at the house for five minutes and then take me to hospital." I looked out through the windscreen, recognised where we were. "It's on the way."

"Why?"

"Because there's something there that will help you catch the person who did this to me." He seemed unconvinced, and I couldn't blame him, because it was a flat-out lie. I added, "I'm going to be out of action for a while so you'll have to make the arrest, but you'll need this thing from the house."

"What thing?"

"It's easier if I just show you."

He thought about it for so long that I thought he was going to miss the turning that led towards the house, but finally he said, "Five minutes."

"Good. Thank you." I relaxed a fraction and almost passed out again. Something occurred to me. "Did you phone this in?"

"You told me not to."

I couldn't remember anything between Cary Grant rushing me, and waking up in the passenger seat of Wally's car. I said, "Where did you find me?"

"By your car."

Nothing. No memory at all. Had I managed to fight the avatar off? Had it been interrupted by someone else? Had it left me for dead? Had it just got bored of hitting me? I tried to open my eyes but my face was swelling up so much that I could barely see as Wally turned the car onto the lane leading up to my house. The lane was narrow and the surface was peppered with potholes; Wally tried to be careful but every time we ran over one it felt as if my body was coming apart. And the lane was a brand new motorway compared to the track which turned off it to my property. Mister Keoshgerian's lorries had left deep ruts in the track and the car bounced along them. Wally slowed us to an agonising crawl and I gritted my teeth and tried to hold myself together for a few more minutes.

Wally finally stopped the car in front of the house. He turned off the engine and looked over at me and the look he gave me made me think that I had underestimated Wally Mole. He was much brighter than anyone imagined. I didn't know if that made him dangerous or not.

"Help me out," I said.

"Can't you just tell me where this thing is and I'll go and get it?" he said.

"You'll never find it," I told him. "Help me out."

He got out, came around the front of the car, and opened the passenger door. He undid my seatbelt and half-lifted me out. I managed to stand, more or less, on my good leg by leaning on the roof of the car, but my heart was pounding and everything kept greying out. I hurt so much I could barely move, let alone walk. I draped an arm across Wally's shoulders and hobbled agonisingly from the car to the front door.

The house was basically an empty shell, just walls and floors and roof. The windows hadn't been installed yet and the front door was just a rectangular hole covered with a sheet of plywood to keep animals out. Wally managed to push it out of the way without dropping me, and we went inside, Wally playing the beam of his torch over the rough unfinished floors and walls

"Living room," I whispered. "First door on the left."

My toes scraped on the bare concrete floor as Wally dragged me through into what I had once hoped would be my living room. He stopped and looked around the bare room. "Now what?" he said.

"Put me on the floor," I said, feeling myself start to drift away again.

"I'm sorry?"

"Sit me down for a minute, Wally. Please."

He lowered me to the floor and I sat there with a ringing in my ears and my vision fading in and out. It occurred to me that I probably really was dying. Broken ribs, broken leg, possible punctured lung, probable concussion at the very least. There was not a single part of me which was not in agony.

I put the palm of my good hand down on the concrete floor and said as clearly as I could, "Augustus Francesco de Palma y Granchester." There was a faint blur of motion across the floor and a square of concrete about two metres on a side turned red, became tenuous and misty, and swept away, exposing a square black hole in the floor. I heard Wally swear and take a step back.

"What's going on?" he asked quietly.

"Magic," I told him. "Help me up." He managed to get me to my feet again. "We have to go down there," I told him, nodding at the hole. "There are sixteen steps and a wall at the bottom."

Wally, being Wally, chose this moment to get stubborn. "Not until you tell me what this is all about, Frank."

I sat there, completely spent, just metres from salvation, and shook my head. "Okay, Walter. Fuck off back to work. I can crawl down there on my own."

"Can you?"

I considered it. "No. I can't. Congratulations, Wally, you've got me by the balls. What you have to ask yourself is, what are you going to do now?"

"What you have to ask yourself," he said, "is what are *you* going to do now."

I tried to smile, but my face no longer responded to orders. "I have always underestimated you, Walter," I told him. "I apologise."

This confused him. "What?"

"Look at it this way," I said. "If you leave me here and go away, you'll never find out what I'm hiding in my cellar."

Wally gave this some thought, while a storm of darkness boiled at the edge of my vision. Finally, I felt him lift me again and start to move towards the trapdoor.

Getting me down the steps was awkward. I bumped my head a couple of times, but it didn't make me feel substantially worse. The lights came on as we reached the second step, and I felt Wally start in surprise, but he kept going, carrying his Sergeant towards who knew what.

At the bottom of the steps was a smooth grey wall. I reached out and put my hand flat against it and waited while the security system tasted my DNA. It seemed to take a long long time.

There was a faint whining sound, like a swarm of bees, just on the edge of audibility, and the wall turned to smoke and blew away.

"Fuck!" Wally shouted.

"Open sesame," I muttered.

In the light of the stairwell I could see a space about ten feet high by twenty long, empty save for a large shadowy shape. "Lights," I said, and the lights in the cellar came on. I mumbled, "Power-up," and heard the faint answering whine of equipment coming alive. It sounded more alive than I did.

The Machine sat in the middle of the floor, gunmetal grey, the size of an armchair, and shaped like a blood platelet. I waved at it. "Over there. Sit me down there."

Wally was suffering from culture shock; he didn't say a word, just dragged me over to the Machine and put me down. He thought it was some weird piece of furniture. He was in for a surprise.

I put my hand against the cool hard surface beneath me. "Medical emergency," I muttered, and the surface puckered under my palm. I heard a scraping noise on the floor, peered myopically across the cellar, and saw Wally backing towards the steps. I said, "Make secure," and the wall came back, sealing us off from the outside world. Up in the living room, the trapdoor was being reconfigured. "Relax," I told Wally. "This won't take long." And I curled up as best I could on top of the Machine and felt myself sinking into it, and then I went away.

Nanotechnology was too good to be true. Once you'd invented it and got it working properly, you wound up using it for everything. You used it to compile your breakfast, your clothes, your house, your car. You couldn't get sick because frantic machines too small to see with the human eye were hurtling around your bloodstream doing things your immune system had only ever dreamed of doing. You compiled avatars to do heavy lifting for you. You lived in a land of Plenty and you could expect to live there for ever because nano had effectively removed the theoretical limit of your lifespan. Famine was abolished. Tyranny was abolished. Paradise.

You could also, if you knew where to look, learn how to compile hunting knives, pistols, assault weapons, nerve gas, microton nuclear munitions and hot viruses. Got a neighbour who turns his sound system up to the pain threshold at four o'clock in the morning when you've got an important meeting at nine? You can turn his house into a smoking hole in the ground that'll set off Geiger counters for the next thousand years. You can call down a plague of boils on his children. You can make his nuts swell up like basketballs. Urban angst? Nanotechnology will help you settle the score.

So it was strictly licenced and regulated, and if that meant the abolition of Tyranny was postponed a little and Paradise was still tantalisingly just out of reach, well that was the price you paid in order to sleep a little more soundly at night.

Except.

It's axiomatic that people can be angry and irrational sometimes, but it's also axiomatic that the same is true for nations. The problem is that when people get angry and irrational the body count is relatively low. When nations do it, they start making weapons of mass destruction to use on their neighbours, or their ideological enemies, or anyone that looks sideways at them.

On the other hand, on a strictly personal level, nanotechnology was the greatest hangover cure ever invented, so swings and roundabouts.

I opened my eyes. I was lying curled up on the floor stark naked next to the Machine, and I felt great. No pain, nothing broken. I took a deep, steady breath and sat up.

"Who are you?"

I pulled a face. I'd forgotten all about Wally. I turned my head and looked at him and said, "I'm Frank Grant."

He waved at the Machine. "You were inside that thing."

"Yes," I admitted. "Yes, I was. Would you believe it's a new supersecret hangover cure?" I watched his face. "No." I sighed. "Worth a try." I patted the Machine. "This, Constable Mole, is *nanotechnology*." Although calling it that was like calling a Bugatti Veyron a 'car'.

Wally looked at the Machine. Then he looked at me. "Let me out of here, Frank."

"Can't do that yet, Wally," I said, getting to my feet. "We need to talk." He took a couple of steps back and I stopped and held out my hands. "I'm not going to hurt you."

"What's going on, Frank?"

"I need to ask you to keep this quiet," I told him. "If anyone finds out about it my career's over."

There was a fairly robust culture of macho at the station. Some of the other officers made fun of Wally because he seemed a little slow, but he wasn't really. He was a bright, decent copper and he took care to think about stuff before he did it, where others just stormed in and relied on testosterone to get the job done. He was also a good friend; I couldn't think of a single officer at the station who would have helped me like this.

He said, "Jesus, Frank. What the fuck are you doing with that thing in your cellar?" He glanced past me at the Machine, and I took a single step forward and tapped him on the forehead with the tip of my index finger. He crumpled so quickly that I barely managed to get my hands under his armpits in time to lower him to the floor. I ordered up some clothes and got dressed, then I dragged Wally across to the Machine, gave it a few commands, pushed his hand into it, and left them to get to know each other.

Back upstairs, I went out and drove Wally's car around to the back of the house and spent an hour or so wiping my blood off the interior. There was a lot of it and in the torchlight I couldn't be sure I'd got it all, but it was the best I could do.

Back in the cellar, the Machine had finished its run and spat Wally out. He was crumpled on the floor beside it, still out cold. I ran a diagnostic, and by the time it was complete he was beginning to stir. I got him to his feet and walked him half-conscious up the stairs and out to the car.

I drove us back into the village, parked outside the police station, and gave Wally a poke. "Walter. Come on, wake up. I'm home."

Wally opened his eyes and looked out of the windscreen. "What?" he said.

"You should go home and get some sleep," I told him. "Or do you want me to drive you?"

He struggled upright against his seatbelt. "What? No." He blinked. "What."

"Don't bother writing up your report right now," I said. "Tomorrow morning will do; just make sure your notes are in order."

"What notes?"

"About Dronfield Farm."

He rubbed his face hard with both hands, trying to wake up. "Right," he said. "Will do."

"Everything was secure," I told him. "No sign of intruders. Bit of a waste of time, really, but I couldn't sleep so I volunteered to go with you."

"Right," he said again. "Thanks for that, Frank." Messing around with his short-term memory like this was a fairly piss-poor way of repaying him for what had been a considerable act of kindness, but I didn't have time for anything more subtle; I still had to go out and retrieve my car.

I made sure he was properly awake, then I got out and watched him drive away. According to his dashboard clock it was almost five in the morning. People around here tended to wake early, getting ready for the commute to Huddersfield and Sheffield, and soon there would be people on the road.

45

There was no time to be subtle about it. I went into the yard at the back of the station, opened one of the sheds, and took out a bicycle, cycled up to the forestry plantation, drove back into the village with the bike in the back of the car, parked around the corner from the station, and returned the bike. I was back in my flat just as the station started to wake up for the morning shift, but I didn't feel remotely tired. I made myself a coffee, opened my laptop, and started to make plans.

Six

One evening couple of days later, I was loading the dishwasher when someone knocked on the door. I opened it and found Pep Song Hing standing in the corridor.

We stood looking at each other for quite some time, Pep and I. I hadn't seen her for a very long while, but she didn't seem to have changed very much, apart from letting her hair grow long enough to wear it in a ponytail. She'd kept her own face, as had I, which at least made recognising each other fairly painless. Finally, I moved aside and let her step into the flat. I closed and locked the door.

She stood in the middle of the living room, looking around and beaming as if delighted by what she was seeing. Then she turned and did the same thing to me. "Francesco," she said.

"Pep," I said from the door.

"You seem to have done well for yourself," she said, and I couldn't tell whether she was being sarcastic or not.

"How did you get in here?" I asked.

"You let me in," she said, putting her denim rucksack down on the floor by her feet and taking off her long black overcoat.

"No," I said patiently. "I meant *in here*."

"Ah," she waved it away. "Your colleagues seem friendly. Aren't you going to offer me a drink?" When I didn't move from where I was she grinned at me. "Back on the wagon, Francesco?" she said. "Well done. Good thing I brought my own, then." And she bent down and rummaged in the rucksack for a moment and came up with a bottle of what I could see, even from here, was a very good and very expensive single malt.

"What do you want?" I said.

"Well, for the moment a *glass* would do," she told me. I nodded at the cupboards and she looked at the kitchen in delight and said, "Oh, a *kitchenette!*" I walked over, took a glass from a cupboard, and handed it to her. "So," she said, looking around the flat again. "*This* is nice."

I stood looking at her. I hadn't expected Regis to send someone, and even if I had it wouldn't have occurred to me that it would be Pep.

She looked at me and screwed up her eyes. "You could at least say something like 'nice to see you, Pep.' After all this time."

Throwing her out was not an option. Quite apart from the fuss it would cause, notwithstanding whatever ruse or gizmo she had used to get in here in the first place, Pep was – had been, anyway – a soldier. Some extremely refined species of Special Forces. She was a foot shorter than me and looked as if a stern look would knock her unconscious, but she could break every bone in my body without getting out of breath. And that was before you took into account any enhancements she might have dialled in. I went over to one of the armchairs and sat down.

"Well, it's nice to see *you*, anyway, Francesco," she said, perching on the sofa and putting the bottle of Scotch down on the cofeetable between us. "How long has it been?"

"You know exactly how long it's been." *Not long enough.*

"And how are you enjoying police work?"

I sighed.

"Hey," she said. "I'm keeping up my end of the conversation. It's not like you're going to ask *me* what I've been up to, is it."

"I think I can guess."

She looked around the flat again, then at me. "Regis showed me your letter," she said. "It sounds as if you have a situation here."

"Have you come to sort it out?"

She shook her head. "I'm just here to deepen the contact, hear you out. Make sure you haven't gone a little gaga out here in the sticks."

"And then what?"

She shrugged. "I imagine we'll wing it. We always do, don't we?"

I said, "There's someone else here. Someone not *us*. I was almost beaten to death by an avatar the other night."

She raised an eyebrow. "How do you know it's not us?"

"There's no beacon. I checked. I'm not stupid, Pep."

She sat there on the edge of the sofa, back straight, hands on her knees, and regarded me soberly for a while. Then she said, "Okay, tell me what happened."

I gave her the bullet points. My first visit to Dronfield Farm, the weird atmosphere at the house, the Cary Grant-skinned avatar, the visit by Sachs and Richmond, my subsequent return to Dronfield Farm and shameful beating.

When I'd finished she shook her head. "My, we *have* been in the wars, haven't we," she said, leaving unspoken the fact that she would have torn the avatar's arm off and clubbed it to bits. She leaned forward, picked up the bottle of scotch, tore off the foil, and twisted out the cork. A delirious smell of whisky mushroomed out and filled the whole flat. She glanced at me. "Sure you won't have one?" she asked, gesturing with the bottle.

"No," I said. "Thank you."

"Okay." She poured herself a measure, recorked the bottle, set it back on the table. "So, you have no evidence that the Hallams are…like us."

"Nothing I could take into court, no. But there's something *wrong* up there. And they've got an avatar hassling them; who would bother doing that if they were natives?"

"If they were in a position to know what it was, they wouldn't want to attract attention to themselves by getting the police involved," Pep pointed out. She took a sip of whisky and smiled. "Mm. That's nice."

That had occurred to me as well, but I shook my head. "Trust me, Pep, there's something dodgy about the Hallams."

"Copper's instinct?" she teased. "Well, maybe you're right. Regis has a theory."

"Oh good."

"Don't be like that, Francesco. You're the one who took himself off into the wilderness; we haven't heard from you since…Well, *ever*. And now all of a sudden you're beating down our door."

"If it's any comfort, you weren't easy to find."

"Yes, well, that was the whole *point*, wasn't it." She regarded me for a little while, then she said, "Okay, when can you come to London? Regis wants a face-to-face."

Where no doubt he had a big house. I spent more time keeping my eye on the financial markets than most police officers, and I thought I could detect certain patterns. Some of the others had been making money the same way I had; a casual observer wouldn't have spotted it, but I knew what to look for.

I said, "Give me a couple of days; I'll have to clear it with my Inspector."

"He thinks we picked up a hitch-hiker."

"A what?"

"He thinks someone came with us."

"That's impossible," I said, although to be honest I had such a basic, entry level grasp of things that it might not only have been possible but perfectly routine.

"Regis will have to explain it to you," she said. "I'm just the messenger."

"You could have emailed me."

"You'd have ignored an email, Francesco." She took another drink. "I read your report about Dronfield Farm."

"You hacked our computer." All of a sudden my mouth seemed to be bone dry and full of saliva at the same time. "It's firewalled."

"Oh come on, Francesco. Feet of the master and all that."

Pep was only a fifth-rate hacker, but I had taught her what little she did know, and she'd be able to go through the craftiest firewall presently available as if it was made of rice paper. Getting into Stockford Police's server would have been no more difficult for her than going into the newsagents', taking a magazine down from the shelf, and opening it. And nobody would ever know she'd been there.

"What about Dronfield Farm?"

"I had a word with the Hallams," she said.

"You did what?"

She took something from her pocket and skimmed it across the tabletop to me. It was an authentic-looking warrant card in the name of Detective Sergeant Susan Ross, and it had her photo on it. "That's illegal," I said. "Unless you really are a Detective Sergeant these days, in which case it's only a serious breach of procedure."

"Francesco," she chided, and she took another drink. "Really."

I scowled. This was why Sachs and Richmond, whoever they were, had been asking about Dronfield Farm – a mysterious and seemingly nonexistent DS wandering about the area could be interpreted in any number of ways, none of them remotely close to the truth. I said,

"You've caused me a lot of trouble, Pep."

"If Regis is right, your little adventures with the local plod are the least of anyone's problems."

"It's not local plod, Pep. It's something else."

She waved it away and actually said, "Whatever."

"All of a sudden we're causing a footprint, and the fact that they responded so quickly means they've been looking for us. And if they're looking for us it means they know who we are." I was talking quickly, trying not to look at the bottle of Scotch. "And if they know who we are it means someone has been careless. Or leaky. Or both."

"They're *natives*, Francesco. Who cares?"

"It's not your life they're digging around in, Pep," I said seriously. "You can't just go wandering around pretending to be a member of CID and hope it won't attract attention."

She gave me a level look which suggested she thought I was over-reacting and I should calm down and have a quiet word with myself. After a little while she said, "Cary Grant."

"It wasn't me."

"Are you sure?"

"I checked."

"*Absolutely* sure."

"Absolutely."

"So," said Pep, "someone else round here must have a Machine."

She already knew the answer to that, of course; she just wanted to see what I would say. I said, "I checked that too. The nearest beacon is more than a hundred kilometres away."

"Do you know who that is?"

I shook my head. "I don't snoop."

She laughed. "You're a *policeman*, Francesco. Snooping is what you *do*."

"I'm not that kind of policeman. I'd like you to go now, Pep."

She thought about that. "Go and see Regis, Francesco. It's important."

"Good to see you and all that, Pep, but please go."

She got up and took her coat and bag from the sofa. "Do you want me to take…?" She nodded at the bottle and the glass.

"Just go, Pep," I said without looking at her. "Don't come back."

She nodded and put on her coat and went to the door. I heard it open, and close again behind her, and for a few moments I heard her footsteps in the corridor outside, and then she was gone and I was on my own and I sat there in perfect silence for what felt like hours, not a thought in my head.

"I'm not sure I can authorise this," John Weller told me the next morning.

"It's not as if I'm doing anything useful here, John," I said.

He grunted and read my request one last time, then laid it on the desk in front of him. "You're supposed to be available if the IOPC need to interview you again."

"I'll only be gone a couple of days."

He gave me a level look. "Is there something I should know, Frank?"

"Like what?"

"You've been here three years and as far as I can remember in all that time you've not gone much further than Sheffield. Now all of a sudden..." He nodded at the sheet of paper.

"That's because I've always been busy. Now I'm just spinning my wheels; I don't see any reason why I can't go."

"I'll have to notify the IOPC," he said.

"Fine. I'm only going to a wedding. I'm not skipping the country."

"They'll say no."

"So don't notify them until tomorrow morning. Lose the paperwork for a few hours."

John had always been straight with me, and I had always been straight with him, apart from the glaring omission of not telling him the whole truth about myself. He said, "'Lose the paperwork'?"

I shrugged. "I didn't do anything wrong, John. You know that, I know that. The *IOPC* probably know that. This is all because Ursula bloody Hinchcliffe's in a snit about us arresting her little darlings. I've had enough of this game."

He sucked his teeth. The need to do everything by the book had a brief battle with his annoyance at Ursula Hinchcliffe messing with his officers' lives.

"I'll put it in the post to them this afternoon," he said finally. "They probably won't get it till Saturday and they might not see it till Monday. By which time you'll be back here." He gave me a look to make sure I understood that this last was an order, not an aspiration.

"I'll be back Sunday evening."

"Yes," he said. "And you'll call me when you get here. Don't disappoint me, Frank."

I had every intention of being back in my flat by about seven on Sunday. Maybe earlier, depending on how things went. "Thank you, John."

Seven

I drove to Leeds, from where I had booked a ticket on the train to York and from there to Edinburgh for my friends' wedding. Instead of getting on the York train, however, I got on the little local hopper to Sheffield. I bought a ticket on the train and I used cash.

In Sheffield, I again used cash to buy a single to London, and I was at St Pancras by lunchtime. As a piece of misdirection it was fairly transparent, but I was counting on John sticking to his word and fudging things so Sachs's people would be unaware of my absence until I was back in Stockford. As far as I could tell, I hadn't been tailed from the station to Leeds, and my countermeasures included a subroutine that rendered my face, posture and gait hard to see on security cameras. Unless I actually physically bumped into Sachs or Richmond or one of their presumed colleagues, I was as sure as I could be that I'd got away with it.

I got the Northern Line to Archway station and walked up the hill past the Whittington Hospital and into Highgate village. It was a cool, dry afternoon here on the heights overlooking central London and Highgate was full of tourists.

Regis lived in a big townhouse on a leafy street off the High Street, a place with a high wall around it and a Regency look to its windows. There was a security box on the wall beside the front gate. I pressed the button and tried not to glare into the camera, and after a few moments there was a click and I was able to push the gate open and step through.

The front door opened as I reached it, and Pep stood there beaming at me. "Francesco," she said. "You made it!"

I pushed past her without saying anything, and found myself in a tiled entrance hall. There were half a dozen doors around the hall, all closed, and a broad stairway leading up to the first floor. Apart from that, and a little antique table bearing a crystal vase full of lilies, it was empty.

"Where is he?" I said as Pep closed the door behind us.

"In the study. This way."

She led me through one of the doors and along a short corridor to another door, where she stopped and knocked. I didn't hear an answering voice, but she opened the door and stepped aside to let me through.

Regis was standing at the window, looking out into the well-tended walled garden beyond. He was tall and straight-shouldered and patrician, and he looked much as I remembered, although the last time I'd seen him his hair had been snow-white, not brown.

"Francesco," he said, stepping out from behind his desk and coming towards me with his hand outstretched and a serious expression on his face. "Thank you for coming at such short notice. Have you eaten?"

"I had something on the train."

He looked past me. "Coffee and sandwiches please, Pep. And could you ask Jan Tyrian to join us?"

"Oh good," I said. "You invited Doctor Strangelove too."

He narrowed his eyes fractionally at me. "You'll keep a civil tongue in your head, Francesco."

"I'll turn round and go home if you keep talking to me like that, Regis."

He smiled. "No you won't. You came here because you want to know what's going on; you won't leave until you at least know that." And he offered me his hand again.

"Fuck you, Regis," I said. But I shook his hand.

"Sit down," he said, waving a hand at a comfy-looking sofa that sat with a couple of armchairs around a low table on the other side of the room. Behind them, a wall of shelves was full of the sort of impressively aged-looking books that interior designers source for their clients in order to make them look Serious and Well-Read. Regis had never read a book in his life; not a paper one, anyway.

He'd done well for himself, but that was probably going to happen wherever he wound up. Regis was that sort of man. He'd been a multi-billionaire when I first met him, and he probably wasn't far off being a billionaire again. Some people just can't be satisfied with having *enough*. They always need to have *more*.

I took one of the armchairs and he sat on the sofa and we didn't make smalltalk because ours was not that sort of relationship. I had worked for him once, and though I hadn't known it at the time that was my ticket here. He thought that meant I owed him something, but as far as I was concerned I'd only been doing my job and if my payment was a little...unusual, that was his problem. We hadn't quite agreed to differ about it, so we sat in silence on our respective soft furnishings until the door opened and Jan Tyrian entered the study.

There was a beat when he spotted me in the armchair, which told me that Regis hadn't bothered to tell him I was coming. Then he recovered and said, with the barest attempt to hide his insincerity, "Francesco. Good to see you."

"Hi," I said.

"He calls himself 'Frank' now," Pep said, coming into the room with a tray.

"Oh?" Jan Tyrian looked at me. "That's...nice." He went over and sat in the other armchair. He was a dapper little man in a white linen suit, a starched collar, and a red tie. It was as if someone had decided to dress a raptor as Tom Wolfe.

Pep came over and put the tray on the table. There were cups and a coffee jug and milk and sugar, and a plate piled high with sandwiches. She winked at me and left again.

Regis said, "Are you in contact with anyone else, Francesc...er, Frank?"

"I wasn't in contact with *anyone* until a couple of days ago, and after I leave here I'd like to go back to not being in contact with anyone."

"That may not be possible," Jan Tyrian said.

"You let me be the judge of what's possible and what isn't." I looked at Regis. "I was perfectly happy where I was until you sent your pet ninja to mess with my head. She said you wanted to talk to me about something. Fine, talk to me. But once you're finished, I'm leaving, and I don't want to see you again. Either of you."

"You'd be dead if it weren't for us," Jan Tyrian snapped.

"Technically, I *am* dead."

"*Technically*, you haven't been born yet."

Regis sighed and raised a hand. "This is all very jolly," he said, "but could you just *not*?"

I looked at them, Regis Colombar and his tame weapons scientist, self-styled saviours of the human race. While Regis' billions had paid for the Project, and Jan Tyrian's expertise with nanotechnology had helped make it possible, I personally thought the people we really had to thank were the thousands of techs and researchers who had worked their hearts out to make it a reality, and had wound up being left behind.

I said, "Did you grass me up to the spooks?"

Regis raised an eyebrow. "Did I what you to the what?"

"I had a visit from a couple of people who smelled like Security; did you nudge them in my direction?"

He shook his head.

"We had a report of a prowler a week or so ago; the householder said the intruder looked like Cary Grant. The Security people seemed quite interested in that, and they weren't particularly subtle about it."

Regis and Jan Tyrian exchanged glances. "Nothing to do with me," said Regis.

"It must be coincidence," Jan Tyrian said. "The natives can't possibly know." Which I thought was one of the stupider things I had ever heard. It was a miracle we hadn't been on the front page of every newspaper on Earth for the past century or so. All it would take was one of us to leak and someone in authority to believe them, although admittedly that last was a bit of a stretch.

The door opened again and Pep stepped into the room. "We have company," she said.

Regis scowled and took out his phone, thumbed up an app, looked at it for a few moments. Then he looked at me. "Are these anything to do with you?" He held up the phone. The screen showed a camera feed of the street outside the house. It was full of police vehicles.

"What should I do?" Pep asked.

Regis sighed. "You'd better let them in," he said. "Knowing the neighbours, this is probably on YouTube already."

"You must think we're really stupid," Sachs told me.

"Actually, I don't," I said. "But I do think there are things you're better off not knowing."

She looked around the room, at Regis and Pep and Jan Tyrian, then returned her gaze to me. It was like a reconstruction of an Agatha Christie country house mystery, Miss Marple gathering the suspects in the drawing room to unmask the murderer, except Sachs was not Miss Marple and we were not murderers.

"I work for the Home Office," she told us.

"Good for you," Regis said, beaming goodwill at her. "And congratulations on tracking us down; it can't have been easy." I was going to have to find out how they'd followed me, at some point, but that wasn't important right now. There were armed tactical officers in the garden and stationed around the property; there was no point trying to style it out.

"There was a suicide three years ago," she said. "In Cardiff. A gentleman named Oxley. Does that ring a bell?" When it was obvious it didn't, she went on, "Local police dealt with it, there was no sign of foul play, but Mr Oxley had no next of kin and during the investigation of his estate certain items of an... anomalous nature were discovered." Oh, excellent. They had a Machine. I wondered whether I had known the person it belonged to.

None of us said anything, just sat there expectantly.

"I won't bore you with the details," Sachs said, "but the items were passed on to us, and our investigations led us to Robert and Leonie Hallam." Beside me, I felt Regis stir slightly. He wanted to be bored with the details.

Sachs wasn't going to indulge us, though. She stood there in front of us and asked, "Where are you from?"

"I'm from Cambridge," I said. "Originally."

"I'm empowered, on behalf of Her Majesty's government, to welcome you to Earth," she went on, "but first I need to know how long you've been here and where your home solar system is."

Pep burst out laughing.

Here's how time travel works:

Time travel does not work. (See also: Here's How Matter Transmission Works)

I don't know why it doesn't work; I'm not a physicist. I know a lot of very smart people tried very hard to make it work and they couldn't.

There was some evidence that one group of researchers had managed to send a speck of platinum the size of a grain of salt two nanoseconds back in time, but the evidence was inconclusive and two nanoseconds was no use to anyone.

What you *can* do – and I can't even begin to pretend to understand this either – is use gravitational waves to transmit a message into the underlying quantum state of the universe and instruct it to sort of spontaneously create matter. The message itself does not travel in time; it actually exists at every point in time and space since the creation of the universe, sort of a cosmic proofreading mark. Which makes time travel seem almost rational.

This is actually an *incredibly* handy, not to mention vaguely godlike, thing to be able to do, and if we'd learned to do it earlier it might have made a difference, but it was just one of hundreds of mad, desperate schemes to combat the Extinction, none of which promised very much success and were, anyway, far too late to do any good. It was so utterly off the wall that Regis had to fund it himself, dumped his entire fortune into the project, but as he told me at the time, dead is dead, whether you're a billionaire or a pauper.

So we transmitted the message and the universe created, every thirty years back as far as the Big Bang, a sort of virtual Machine. Most of them only existed for the tiniest fraction of a second, but some, the smallest percentage, lasted long enough to create a copy of themselves out of native feedstock before falling back into their quantum state. And the copies created us.

"Did it never occur to you to wonder why an extraterrestrial would want to join an English provincial police force?" I asked.

"Why would anyone?" Sachs said grumpily.

I looked at the window. It was getting dark outside; the police vehicles had gone, although a number of officers remained in the house. The Met would put out a press release saying it had been a false alarm, bad intelligence resulting in an anti-terror operation, but Regis would still have to move; the neighbours would be watching him from now on.

After the initial shock and awe, which had not in all honesty been terribly shocking or awesome, Sachs and her people had split us up. I had wound up in an upstairs bedroom with only an armed officer for company. I'd tried to engage her in conversation about the Job, but she wasn't inclined to talk so I'd spent my time examining the truly awful paintings which hung on the walls until Sachs got round to me. When she did make an appearance, she seemed a little shaken, from which I deduced that Regis and the others had told her at least a fraction of the truth about us.

I said, "You were prepared to believe we were aliens, how much harder is this to believe?" It was obvious Sachs still didn't quite believe it. Little green men pretending to be human? Sure, why not? Time travellers from the twenty-sixth century? Not so much. "Although I'm more curious as to why you thought we *were* aliens. Was Oxley modded? Carrying some extra bits? Not quite baseline human?"

"Perhaps you could help us with that," she said.

"Not my area of expertise. Sorry."

"Just out of interest, what *is* your area of expertise, Frank? You're not really a police officer, are you?"

I really was a police officer, and it annoyed me that she was glossing over that, but I knew what she meant. "I do system design. Computer security." Although that was a bit like Robert Oppenheimer telling an eleventh century swordsmith that he worked on weapons.

"So why join the police service?"

I shrugged. "I had to do *something*. I like it; it lets me help people." And now I wouldn't be able to do it any more. The Job, Stockford, John Weller, my house, that was all over. The comfortable, useful little life I'd made for myself had blown away, and that made me angry. "What connected Oxley to us?"

"Some of his neighbours said they'd seen someone who was the spitting image of Cary Grant coming and going from his house in the weeks leading up to his death. We didn't know what to make of it, but we set up a keyword alert and we'd almost forgotten about it when it popped up in your report, and that led us to you, and you led us here."

"I was really careful."

"You were, and we were very impressed. But we're very good at our job and there are more of us than you. You never stood a chance."

I hadn't really had a choice about mentioning Leonie Hallam's description of the intruder; she'd given the same description when she made her initial call and it was in the log. It would have looked suspicious if I'd left it out. It was just pure dumb chance that I'd been the one sent to respond to the call. Otherwise Sachs and her people might have passed me by.

"So," I said. "What happens now? We've committed no crime; you have no right to hold us, we're not required to cooperate."

"Technically, you're illegal immigrants."

"Good luck trying to deport us."

"You can't go back?"

"Doesn't work that way," I said. "It was a one-way trip."

"What are you *doing* here?"

"We're refugees." Which was true, but didn't even remotely begin to cover everything. "And please don't ask me what we're refugees from, because I can't tell you. I can't tell you anything about the future because it would change this timeline." This was bullshit, and it didn't matter anyway because the timeline *needed* to be changed. Anything that stopped events leading to the Extinction was a good thing, as far as I was concerned.

We sat looking at each other for a while, each of us wondering what was going through the other's mind. She said, "I need to know if your presence here represents some kind of threat."

I shook my head. "We've been taking care not to make waves since we arrived." Apart from using ancient stock market data to make ourselves rich. "We just want to be left alone."

That option obviously no longer existed, but Sachs chose to set it aside for the moment. She said, "What's happening at Dronfield Farm? Are the Hallams part of your group?"

"I don't know. The Machines are all equipped with beacons, so we can find each other if we have to – and most of us seem not to want to. There's no beacon at the farm, or anywhere in the area."

"Could they have turned it off?"

"Sure, but why would they?"

"You didn't recognise each other?"

"No, but that doesn't mean anything. I didn't meet everyone who was coming here. Anyway, an hour or so in their Machine and they could look like anyone they wanted to."

She thought about that. "If they're completely blameless, why was an avatar wandering around their farm, though?" She'd obviously been picking up bits of terminology from the others.

"That's what I've been wondering. An avatar's basically a semi-sentient machine; we use them for hard physical work. The fact that it looks like Cary Grant doesn't mean anything. The Machines have a menu of hundreds of different designs; the Cary Grant one was just in fashion when we left. It's the first one someone would think of using."

Sachs sat and looked at me for a while again. I could see she was struggling, but I actually thought she was coping pretty well, notwithstanding she'd been forced to take a sudden hundred and eighty degree turn after believing we were the advance party of an alien invasion. "What I can tell you," I said, "because it won't change the timeline at all, is that people are just as stupid in five hundred years as they are now. If you keep that in mind you'll do all right."

She sighed. "You're all going to have to be properly debriefed, but first I need to know if we have to do anything about the Hallams."

I thought about it. "Yes," I said finally. "Yes, we do."

"How many of you are there, by the way?" Sachs asked.

"I don't know," I told her. "And that's the honest truth; I just don't know."

She let it drop. We were sitting in her car in the little patch of Forestry Commission plantation that bordered Dronfield Farm, drinking coffee from a thermos and eating slightly stale croissants we'd bought at a service station on the M1 on the way up from London.

"You ought to let Jan Tyrian have a look at Oxley's Machine," I said, something occurring to me. "It should have self-destructed when he died." She glanced at me. "Nothing spectacular; it should just have decompiled itself. If it didn't, someone carried out quite a fundamental hack on it."

"Is that significant?"

"It's not something you'd do by accident."

She brushed pastry crumbs from her lap and took a sip of coffee. "What can we expect here?"

"If they *are* part of our group, there will be countermeasures. They should be nonlethal."

"But if someone's been hacking the Machines…"

"Quite." I kept thinking of what Pep had said, about Regis's theory that we'd picked up a hitch-hiker. I hadn't seen him since Sachs gatecrashed our meeting, so I hadn't had the chance to ask him what that meant.

"How bad could it be?"

"Pretty bad." We'd stopped off at my house and Sachs had boggled for twenty minutes or so while she watched my Machine compile some gear. Ideally, I would have liked Pep to be there too, for support, but Pep was in the doghouse because she'd grown bored waiting for Sachs to interview her and she'd dislocated her guard's shoulder for something to do.

"Well, we'd better be about it then," said Sachs. She opened her door and tipped the remains of her coffee onto the ground.

"Yup," I said, getting out of the car and slinging my rucksack over one shoulder.

We walked through the trees until we reached the edge of the field, where we paused and surveyed Dronfield Farm.

"Looks deserted," Sachs said, lowering her binoculars.

"Looks that way," I said. I unzipped my rucksack and took out a black polyhedron the size of a golfball. I threw it as hard as I could, and it landed just inside the wire surrounding the farm. I consulted a readout on my tablet, then led the way across the field to the fence. I threw another couple of sensors into the yard, checked again, then climbed through the fence and walked up to the house, Sachs following a couple of footsteps behind. If she was at all anxious about doing any of this – and she'd be inhuman if she wasn't – she was hiding it remarkably well.

"They've gone," she said, nodding at the front door, which stood slightly ajar.

I held the tablet up and turned in a slow circle. The only lifesigns it picked up were mine and Sachs's. I took out another couple of sensors and pitched them through the gap between the door and the frame, bouncing them off the wall inside and along the hall. I looked at the tablet, then nudged the door open with my toe.

"Well," I said.

Eight

It would have been nice to tell the inhabitants of the Twenty-First Century that there was a bright future among the stars waiting for their great-grandchildren, but there wasn't. Humanity had died – *would* die – mostly on the planet of its birth, still trying to make sense of what had gone wrong.

I often thought that we were perhaps not meant to be a spacefaring race. That kind of effort takes huge amounts of money, the amounts you only get when hundreds of nations get together and cooperate with a single purpose, and that never happened. Not once.

Mankind's Future In Space comprised the many habs of the orbital Halo, a base on the Moon, an admittedly ambitious terraforming effort that had left Mars even more uninhabitable than it had started out, asteroid-mining stations on Ceres and Vesta, and a heavily-shielded robot laboratory orbiting Europa – basically a solid-state observatory the size of a fridge. How on Earth could I tell anybody that? The Human Race doesn't even make it as far as Saturn – oh, and by the way, we all die screaming in 2572.

There were those who believed the Extinction was self-aware. I didn't buy that, myself, but I could see why people would think that. It was easier to blame a malign sentience for what was happening, rather than being more honest and blaming ourselves for creating the catastrophe. No one knew where it had come from. The presumption was that some nation or other had developed it from existing nanotechnology and then either released it by accident or, having become annoyed with another nation, used it deliberately.

In the end, though, it didn't matter whether it was sentient or not. It moved across the face of the Earth like a pandemic, decompiling everything it touched, and nothing we did could stop it. Eventually it would break down the entire Solar System.

Armstrong Base succumbed to the Extinction. Lagrange One blew up, nobody knew whether it was a particularly catastrophic accident or mass suicide. When we left, the people in the Belter colonies and those aboard Gateway Station were still alive, so technically the Human Race hadn't become extinct. It merely had to get used to the idea that the Galaxy had just become a very lonely place to live. And anyway, it was only a matter of time.

There had not, it goes without saying, been any way to evacuate Earth, even if there had been anywhere to put the evacuees. Mankind faced up to its death the way it had always faced the really big issues. Badly.

And several thousand of us ran away. Kind of.

"Some of the Machines have been glitching recently," said Jan Tyrian. "It's nothing serious and it's easily fixed, but it's a worry because we rely on them so much."

"Speak for yourself," I said, and then I remembered what I had last used my Machine for. I leaned forward and took one of the sandwiches. I peeled the bread apart. Pressed chicken breast, a smear of cranberry jelly, a couple of bits of lettuce. I reassembled the sandwich and put it back on the platter in the middle of the table.

"When it became obvious that it wasn't just one or two Machines, we decided to map their beacons, and Jan Tyrian's been visiting them and running updates," said Regis. "We estimate around fifteen percent of them are affected – and that's just the ones that are accessible to us here and now; people are going to keep on arriving for the next hundred years or so and we can't do anything about them until they get here."

We were sitting in a bleak, windowless room deep in the bowels of an anonymous building just off Northumberland Avenue. The food was awful and the daylight emulation lighting was giving me a headache. The others looked none the worse for whatever they had been through since I'd last seen them. Sachs and I had left the Hallams' deserted house to a search team and come back to London for a council of war, or at least a council to try and work out what it was that we were at war with. I'd spent a couple of hours with a computer artist, coming up with likenesses of the Hallams for circulation to the police, and that was worth a try, but if they had access to a Machine – and there was a large void under Dronfield Farm which the authorities had still not managed to break into – the chances were they didn't look like the Hallams any more.

"The information which created the Machines in the first place was *ferociously* complex and fragile," Jan Tyrian went on. "We expected errors – there was only a ten percent chance that it would work at all – but we expected them to be evenly distributed instead of randomly affecting a small number of Machines."

"You're thinking sabotage," I said.

He shrugged. "It's one possibility. I ran diagnostics on the Machines I checked, and I found an anomaly, way back in the event logs shortly after they were compiled."

I felt cold fingers walking up the back of my neck. "Is this going where I think it's going?"

"Oh, you'll never guess this one," Regis said. "Not in a million years."

Jan Tyrian looked at him and gave him a little frown of annoyance. "The Machines are programmed to do a number of production runs as part of their boot-up routine, from various inanimate objects to a number of avatars, before going on to their main job, which is compiling us. The test jobs are decompiled for reuse of feedstock, but in every machine that glitched I found a deficit. Missing feedstock."

"The avatars decided they didn't want to go back in the soup," Pep said.

This time, Jan Tyrian glared at her. "It really isn't funny."

She bugged her eyes out at him. "Some of it is."

I looked at Jan Tyrian. Then I looked at Pep. Then I looked at Jan Tyrian. "So, we've got a bunch of glitching Machines and they've all, what, compiled spurious avatars?"

Regis and Jan Tyrian looked at each other. "An avatar is minimally sentient," Jan Tyrian said. "It's supposed to wait for instructions, not take off on its own. It would be like a production line making one extra car and the car deciding to drive away of its own volition. No, I think they've been making spurious *people*."

Nobody said anything.

"There's no way to check this as a fact, unless we can find one of them," said Regis, "but it looks as if someone inserted some subroutines into the original message, the one that caused the Machines to spontaneously self-compile."

"Which is *enormously* complicated, should have been impossible, and could have fucked things up for all of us," Jan Tyrian said. "I can only think of half a dozen people in the world who could even have thought to try it, and two of *them* are here already."

I sat back in my over-designed and uncomfortable chair and rubbed my eyes. Beside me, Sachs remained silent. It was some time since she'd said anything because a lot of it was going straight over her head, but everything was being recorded and she could have it explained to her by experts later. The important thing was that we were talking.

"What I'm thinking," Regis said, mostly for Sachs's benefit, "is that we built a lifeboat and somebody climbed aboard without us realising."

"Is that a bad thing, particularly?" Sachs asked.

I took my hands away from my eyes. "I told you, people are just as stupid five hundred years from now. We had to be selective. There were some people you wouldn't want running around here."

"There was actually a rigorous programme of testing," Regis told her. "We turned a lot of people away." He didn't mention that I had almost been among them, and I didn't mention that I'd hacked into the database and looked at my test results.

"Criminals," Sachs said. "You're telling me there are criminals here from five hundred years in the future."

There was a long, awkward silence. Eventually, Jan Tyrian said, "I'm afraid there's no way of knowing. I can only make the vaguest guess at how it was accomplished in the first place. They were desperate, certainly, but we all were." This earned him a hard stare from Regis. The very last thing we wanted the natives to know about was the Extinction.

She looked around the table. "What have you done?"

"I saved my people," Regis said with such magisterial gravity that I almost guffawed. "If someone subverted the project, that's not my fault."

'My people' was anyone who could pony up a large enough contribution to the costs of the research project, salted with a handful of people Regis thought would be of some use to him in the twenty-first century. What we had actually done was send the top one percent of the world's wealthiest kleptocrats back in time. They were not, on the whole, the most trustworthy people in the solar system. But Sachs didn't need to know that. They'd all passed the tests, even if Regis had put his finger on the scales on the behalf of some of them, and as far as I could tell they were all behaving themselves, making themselves unobtrusively rich again and not bothering anyone. This other group, though, the ones who'd climbed into the lifeboat…well, there was no way to know. They were rich and they were desperate and there was at least one genius among their number.

I said, "May we see the autopsy report on Mr Oxley, please? And an inventory of everything that you found?"

"Do you think that would help?" asked Sachs.

"It can't hurt. In fact, if you could let me see the whole file on his suicide and your investigation it might be useful."

"Okay. I'll see about that." She made a note on the pad in front of her. "Anything else?"

I hadn't had a chance for a quiet chat with Regis before this meeting, but from their body language I assumed that he and Sachs were involved in some kind of negotiation regarding our future. There was nothing I could do about that, so I might as well forget it until it became relevant to me.

I said, "Somewhere to live might be nice." There were noises of agreement around the table, except from Regis, who I presumed had already made provisions for himself.

She frowned fractionally and made another note. "I'll see about that too. Don't expect the Ritz, though, we're on a budget."

"I had a place to live," I pointed out. "Before you came crashing into my life."

She regarded me levelly for a few moments, then she made another note.

"And if you think you have us over a barrel, you ought to remember that we have capabilities that you can't begin to imagine." Everyone looked at me. "So if you want our cooperation it might be best if you treat us with some respect, or we'll just walk out of here and you'll never see us again."

Sachs narrowed her eyes at me. "Point noted," she said evenly.

"Thank you. Now, could we *please* have some decent food in here?"

"'Capabilities that you can't begin to imagine'?" Regis said quietly to me later.

Unless we were carrying a lot of mods, we were indistinguishable from the natives, disappointingly baseline. "It'll keep them on their toes," I told him.

"I don't want these people antagonised," he said. "Things are very delicate at the moment."

I looked at him. "Oh, I'm sorry, Regis," I said. "I've lost my home and my job and pretty much everything I've worked for – and I *have* worked, not sat on my fat arse indulging in insider dealing – since I got here. I apologise for being *antagonistic*."

He gave me a long-suffering look and lowered his voice even further. "They're chomping at the bit to stick us into NMR scanners and take blood and tissue samples and Christ knows what all else," he said. "Basically everything short of actual vivisection. At the moment I've managed to talk them out of it, but that's going to change if we piss them off. Seriously, Francesco. Just behave."

"Fuck you, Regis," I said, and I walked away.

Nine

My Machine spat me out, naked and fully conscious and screaming, on the third floor of a disused parking garage in Leamington Spa at half past three on an October morning in 2009, five hundred years or so before the Extinction. Simultaneously, several thousand other Machines in deserted places around the world and at various points in human history were ejecting their creations, each one built to specifications embedded in the original quantum message. I had no idea how all that had been achieved; at that point the only thing that mattered was that it *had* been achieved.

The parking garage had been abandoned for some time, waiting for demolition which kept being put off because the economy was in freefall. The Machine set up defences, then it made me clothes and food and a cosy little pod to sleep in. It also made me a terminal, and I set about hacking into various databases and backstopping an identity for myself. After a few days, the Machine made me currency and various bits and pieces of identification, and I set out to have a look around.

First priority was shelter. I solved that by looking at the cards in newsagents' windows until I found one that looked, from its faded biro writing and general state of shabbiness, to have been there for some time. I made an appointment to see it, and the landlord was so relieved when I said I'd take it and pulled out a wad of cash to cover the deposit and the first six months' rent that he didn't even bother to look at my carefully-backstopped references. Two days later, with the Machine disguised as a large steamer trunk, I moved in.

After that, it was just a case of sitting tight and collecting pieces of identity. A new passport, to replace the phantom one which I had convinced the Home Office database had just expired, arrived, as did utility bills, and I used those to open bank accounts. In the evenings, I sat and wandered through the charmingly primitive security of various databases and filled in Frank Grant's backstory.

All of this would have been difficult or flat-out impossible for one of the natives, but I had a number of advantages. Firstly, the Machine took care of all my needs, from food to a top-of-the-line laptop. Secondly, I was a security consultant from the twenty-sixth century, which as far as the computer systems of the twenty-first century were concerned meant I was basically a wizard. Thirdly, I had done my homework in nitpicking detail. Preparation is everything.

Sometimes, late at night, I thought about Francesco, the original Frank. He had not travelled in time; he'd simply been copied and reproduced by the weirdest 3D printer ever imagined. Eventually quarantine would have failed somehow, the Extinction would have reached the Halo, the habs would have gone dark one by one, and Francesco would have faced death along with the rest of the human race. I presumed he faced it blind drunk.

After a week or so of sleeping on a camp bed in one of the offices of the building on Northumberland Avenue, I was told to gather together my things – which amounted to a toothbrush and a razor and a couple of changes of clothes provided by Sachs's people – and I was taken down to the garage beneath the building and invited to get into a black SUV with smoked windows.

I had never spent a lot of time in London, so, apart from Trafalgar Square and a glimpse of King's Cross station as it went by, I had no idea where we were. Neither the driver nor the three large minders who accompanied us seemed inclined to tell me.

Finally, we pulled into a side street and went down a ramp into another underground garage, and from there a lift took us up six floors to a little carpet-floored vestibule that smelled of wood polish and Brasso. There were two big, old-fashioned doors here. One had an EMERGENCY EXIT sign on it, the other the number 54 and a column of locks. One of the minders took a bunch of keys from his pocket and spent a couple of minutes opening the door, and then we stepped into my new home.

It was a big flat with high ceilings and thick walls and wood-block floors and utilitarian, slightly-worn furniture. It was one of those places where there is a Residents' Committee and you have to apply in writing if you want to put a hook in the wall to hang a painting. The bathroom was tiled like an old public lavatory and the bath was a huge cast-iron monstrosity with a confusing-looking mixer tap/shower arrangement. The most modern thing in the flat was the retro-style SMEG fridge-freezer in the kitchen, which stood in a corner like an invader from the 1950s. I could imagine Hercule Poirot living here, if he lowered his standards catastrophically.

"There'll be one of us in here and outside all the time, sir," said one of the minders. I lifted the net curtain back from one of the windows and found myself looking down five floors into a busy London street. Directly opposite was another big block dating from the early years of the twentieth century, a wall of windows and shallow balconies. "We'd rather you didn't do that, sir, actually," the minder added.

I let the curtain fall back and looked sourly around the living room, noting the things which were *not* there. No telephone or visible phone line, no television, no little ping in my head to denote a live wifi hotspot. I said, "If you think I'm going to spend an open-ended length of time cooped up in here you're crazy."

"We're only ten minutes' walk from Regent's Park," said the minder. "I'm sure we can work something out, once you're settled. I'm Andrew, by the way."

He looked like a rugby player who had graduated with a 2:2 in Classics from a minor Oxford college. "Frank." We shook hands.

"This isn't such a bad place," he told me. "Concierge service, health club in the basement, nice gardens at the back. I've seen worse."

Compared to my flat at the station in Stockford, it had a certain faded grandeur, but at least there I'd been able to come and go as I pleased. "I'll need clothes," I said. "And toilet things. And food."

Andrew nodded. "I'll be happy to organise that, if you'll just give me a list." He looked round the flat. "In the meantime, I understand there's a terrific shawarma place round the corner on Baker Street. How about we get a takeaway?"

Central London property prices being what they were, the flat was probably worth well over a million pounds, but it was still a prison, and I set out to become a good prisoner. I didn't make waves about having to share it with Andrew or one of the other minders. I didn't comment on the fact that someone was sitting in an armchair in the vestibule outside twenty-four hours a day. I didn't even mention that the door to the emergency stairs was kept locked at all times. I sat and made smalltalk with my jailors and I worked my way through a dogeared stack of airport thrillers which had probably seen service in a number of similar safe houses. After a couple of weeks, I was deemed harmless enough to be allowed out for a walk every few days. Accompanied by Andrew and several other minders, I walked in Regent's Park and up onto Parliament Hill, and one afternoon we all went to the Zoo. I had a growing sense that I was surplus to requirements, that I had fulfilled some purpose but still needed watching. I tried not to let my annoyance show, but I got snappy a couple of times, and afterward my walks were suspended for a few days.

Three days a week, I was taken down to the garage and driven back to Northumberland Avenue to meet with Sachs and the others. I could judge by everyone's body language how well Regis' *negotiations* with the British authorities were going. Sometimes things were tense, sometimes they were relaxed. Things seemed to have stalled.

One morning, after coffee and smalltalk, Sachs handed me a battered briefcase. I opened it and saw a number of fat folders stuffed inside.

"That's everything you asked for," she said. "I'm sorry, but you'll have to read it here; I can't let you take it out of the building. And if you want to make notes you'll have to surrender them at the end of the day."

It was better than ploughing through yet another Arthur Hailey. I took myself off to a little office down the corridor from the meeting room, and there, with another minder standing outside the door, I took the folders out of the briefcase and arranged them on the desk in front of me.

There were four of them, marked with stripes of varying colours denoting levels of confidentiality. There were little holes on the front covers where, I presumed, reading lists had been stapled and then removed so that I couldn't memorise the initials of whoever had been there ahead of me. I glanced quickly through their contents, rearranged the folders in what seemed to be chronological order of panic, and started at the beginning.

Andrew Graham Oxley had been found dead at his home in Spicer Street, Cardiff, three and a half years ago. It was a hot midsummer and his next door neighbour had begun to notice an unpleasant smell coming from somewhere. She hadn't seen Oxley for a couple of weeks and eventually she put two and two together and called the police. The officers who attended the scene checked the house both front and back and found all windows shut and all exterior doors locked. Looking through the windows, they could see no signs of a struggle, no sign of a body, but yes, there was a suggestive smell, so they brought in a local locksmith to let them in through the back door.

They found Mr Oxley in an upstairs bedroom at the back of the house, in an advanced state of decomposition. He was lying face-down on the floor, possibly having had second thoughts at the last minute. There were two empty packets of sleeping tablets on the bedside table. There were photographs of the scene, which I glanced at and put to one side.

Mr Oxley was a stereotype. Lived alone, kept himself to himself, was polite but not overly friendly with his neighbours. Nobody could remember quite when they'd last seen him, but no one thought he'd been particularly depressed or particularly happy. His immediate neighbour, a Mrs Balcon, remembered that he had recently received several visits from a well-dressed gentleman who, she said, strongly resembled Cary Grant, but she hadn't seen the gentleman for some weeks. Attempts to identify 'Cary Grant' went nowhere, and eventually petered out due to lack of resources.

The body was taken to the mortuary of a local hospital, where an autopsy was performed. Allowing for decomposition, it found that Mr Oxley had been an adult male of between forty and fifty years, a little under two metres tall and in good health, deceased for between one and two weeks. Toxicology results were rendered inconclusive due to the state of the body, but the coroner eventually ruled that Mr Oxley had taken his own life.

Meanwhile, investigations to track down next of kin were proving unproductive. Mr Oxley seemed to have no living family, and few, if any, close friends – no one who looked like Cary Grant, anyway. For the past eight years he had worked as an accountant with a small engineering firm on the other side of the city. His employers said he was quiet, conscientious, otherwise forgettable.

Eventually, Mr Oxley's estate passed into the hands of the courts, who employed a local firm to clear his house. In the course of the clearance several sets of keys were found which did not fit any of the locks which Mr Oxley would have encountered during his life. People collect keys, down the years; most families will have half a dozen or so which no longer have any use – keys to long-lost bicycle locks or suitcases, keys to former homes which were somehow not handed over to new owners – but someone actually made an effort to try and fit Mr Oxley's keys to their locks.

I was on to the next folder now, a much higher security classification. It seemed that everyone involved with the investigation into Andrew Oxley's death had behaved with admirable professionalism, particularly the clerk who had gone an extra mile and actually identified one of the sets of keys as belonging to a lock-up garage under a railway arch a few minutes' drive from Spicer Street. When the clerk visited the lock-up he discovered it to be empty apart from something he described as 'a large grey ceramic sculpture'. There were photographs of the sculpture, both *in situ* and later in a laboratory at Cardiff University, where it was taken in an attempt to ascertain what it was. The Machine – because that was what it was – seemed completely inert, a solid block of... something, no one could be quite sure, and that was when the authorities began to take a keener interest.

A senior pathologist was invited to take another look at Mr Oxley's autopsy results and some of the samples taken from his body, and she discovered what appeared to be elevated levels of unusual elements in the samples – breakdown products from nanotechnology which had decompiled when their host died, but the authorities weren't to know that. Additionally, she found anomalous structures in Oxley's long bones, overlooked during the first autopsy because all the original pathologist had been trying to do was establish the cause of death.

At this point, everything moved to the next folder, the one I presumed would result in a life sentence if it was leaked to the Press. The cover was covered in stripes and stamped with dire warnings.

Mr Oxley's body and the Machine, and a few other odds and ends from his home, vanished into a government research unit on the outskirts of Watford. The Machine was a bust; it just sat there and didn't react to anything. But the scientists had more luck with Mr Oxley, who was progressively disassembled and subjected to intense analysis.

A parallel investigation was going on into Mr Oxley's background, and for several decades it seemed entirely blameless. Beyond that, though, it began to throw up anomalies, little things which a cursory – or even a moderately stringent – check would have either overlooked or dismissed as clerical errors. There were paper documents – difficult to insert into the record – missing, school photographs which should have included a happy smiling young Oxley but which did not. I recognised those signs, and so did the Security Service investigators. Andrew Graham Oxley was a legend, a fable, a man of paper.

The obvious conclusion was that he had been a sleeper, an officer of a foreign intelligence agency placed in Britain against future need. If so, he had been here a very long time, and that made people sit up and take notice because he probably wasn't alone.

The spectre of a cell of long-term agents-in-place didn't last long; it was superceded by an even worse nightmare.

Which took me to the final folder. This one, judging by the stamps and stripes on the cover, required me to shoot myself immediately after reading it.

The final scientific report on Andrew Graham Oxley concluded that, although he had presented as a human being, he had actually been quite some distance from baseline. Although his mods had decompiled when he died, there were enough structures left behind for the pathologists and researchers to identify a number of what they originally thought were deformations or mutations.

I read the final page of the report, the one where the researchers came to the unwilling and frankly outrageous conclusion that Mr Oxley had not been human, that he had in fact been an extraterrestrial, then I tidied up all the papers notes and memos and photographs and put them back into their various folders. I put the folders back in the briefcase and I went to look for the others.

"Well," I said, "the first thing is that he didn't kill himself, at least not with sleeping pills. He would have had all the standard medical nano and you can't turn that stuff off or modify it; it would have detoxified him whether he wanted it to or not."

"You think he was murdered?" asked Sachs.

"I don't know. There's too much in the pathology that's inconclusive – he was pretty far gone when he was found." I looked at the briefcase sitting on the table in front of Sachs. "I *can* tell you he was here a long time. This wasn't the first time he'd cooked up an identity." I watched Regis and the others as I said this, but no one stirred. "He was good at it," I went on. "He knew his way around databases and he knew what to do once he was inside them. If he hadn't died, nobody would have been any the wiser. Eventually he'd have decided to leave his job, he'd have moved away, altered his appearance, and started again somewhere else."

Sachs made a note. "Cary Grant?"

I shrugged. "I can't even begin to guess. Maybe he compiled an avatar to do some work for him somewhere, maybe he just wanted someone to talk to."

"So Oxley's a dead end?" Sachs said. Then she winced. "Sorry. Bad choice of words." This time I saw Regis smirk.

"Unless there's a clue in his Machine," I said, looking at Jan Tyrian.

He seemed to take a moment or so to realise I was addressing him. He looked around the table. "I'm afraid it's locked," he said. "Powered down, completely inert. I couldn't get it to respond. Sorry."

"It should have crumbled and blown away," I said.

"Yes," he said. "Yes, that may be significant, but without diagnostics I can't explain it." We looked each other in the eye for a few moments, then he looked away and started to doodle on the notepad in front of him.

"I suspect he's not relevant," Regis piped up. "An unfortunate coincidence."

"A bit *too* fucking unfortunate, considering where we've ended up," I said.

"We were advised there could be some suicides," he pointed out.

"Yes," I said. "Yes, we were." I remembered a briefing from a creepy little psychiatrist. Loneliness, survivor guilt, all the happy problems I had to look forward to. He'd said there was an expectation of maybe one or two percent suicides, a slightly higher percentage of psychological problems. These were, though, he said, people with strong egos, people with a high survival instinct; suicide wasn't expected to be a major factor. What he'd actually meant was that we were about to send the cream of the apex selfish back to the twenty-first century and they couldn't give a shit about anyone but themselves. At least three of the people around this table fitted that description.

Later that evening, there was a discreet knock on the door. Andrew, who was babysitting me that week, went to answer it, and a few moments later Sachs came into the living room.

"Hi," she said.

"Hello," I said, putting aside the Arthur Hailey I'd been reading.

"I wondered if you'd like to go out to dinner."

"What's the occasion?"

"No occasion," she said. "I thought you might feel like getting out of here for a couple of hours."

"Did you have somewhere in mind?"

"There's a little Italian place I go to in Marylebone sometimes. I thought we could try that."

I sat there looking at her for a few moments, thinking, then I said, "Sure. Why not?"

The little Italian place turned out to be tucked away down a mews off Marylebone High Street, and it was almost deserted. Andrew and one of the other minders walked us there and then went off to a nearby pub because they weren't cleared for any conversation Sachs and I might have.

The owner seemed to know Sachs, kissed her on both cheeks and led us to a secluded table near the back of the restaurant, away from the half-dozen or so other diners. There were just enough people here, the background music just loud enough, that no one would be able to overhear us. I wondered what Sachs was playing at.

In the event, she kept the conversation unclassified until we'd got through our starters, chatting about the weather, current events, how I was finding life in the flat. When our main courses arrived, though, she said, "Why did you do it?"

I looked up from my *coda alla vaccinara*. "Do what?"

"You didn't actually *go* anywhere, did you," she said. "The way Regis describes it you all travelled back in time, but it's more like you just took a lot of selfies and emailed them somewhere."

"Oh." I took a mouthful of food. It was really good.

"Please tell me if you don't want to talk about this," she said.

"It's okay," I said. "It's just hard to explain."

"What I don't understand is why you'd do it," she went on. "It must have cost a fortune. All that time and effort, and you'd never know if it had worked or not."

"Some of us thought Regis had got a message from his earlier self," I said. "A postcard from the twenty-first century. 'Hi, wish you were here, but you *won't* be unless you build *this* device.' And he talked a lot of very rich people into funding it, in return for being sent back themselves." I shrugged. "We were desperate. We had nothing to lose."

"That's not an answer," she pointed out. "'We were desperate, we had nothing to lose.' How many people have you arrested who tried that argument?"

I chuckled. "Not as many as you'd think."

She poked at her *timballo Alberoni* with her fork. "I was watching you earlier," she said. "When you told us that Oxley might have been here for a very long time. You were watching the others to see how they reacted."

Well spotted. I thought about it. "It sounds counterintuitive, but although we all arrived at the same time, we didn't all arrive *in* the same time," I said. "We were given a choice of destination and most of us decided to cluster around now, the first quarter of the twenty-first century. I don't know why, it's hardly regarded as a golden age." I saw the look on her face. "Sorry, but it's just not."

"Okay," she said.

"Some people decided they wanted to arrive later, twenty-second, twenty-third century. So they won't be here for a while. But some – maybe a dozen or so – wanted to arrive *earlier*. Two or three hundred years earlier."

"So they've already been here for two or three centuries."

I nodded. "I don't know why they'd want to do that; I can't see any particular advantage in slogging your way through life for a hundred years or so before you even get to the Industrial Revolution. But assuming they managed to survive that long they'd be the oldest people on the planet. Very old and very private and very, very wealthy. Not people you'd want to mess with." And probably, I thought, just a little bit weird by now. "I've never met any of them, but back in the early days, when I'd just arrived and I was still getting my bearings, I used to hang out with a couple of people who'd heard of them. They called them *Elders* and they had a lot of wild stories about them, how they were running everything from behind the scenes, how they were richer than God, wiser than Zeus. You know the kind of thing. Illuminati stuff."

"And you think Oxley was one of them?"

"I don't know. Seems unlikely, a hugely-rich, hugely-old, hugely-powerful person living in a terraced house in Cardiff and working as an accountant, but you can never tell. I thought I'd throw it into the conversation, see what happened."

"And nothing happened."

"Not a dickybird. I thought I'd at least get a raised eyebrow but it was as if hadn't said anything at all."

"Which in itself is suggestive."

"Yes, I'm just not sure how. I'm still working on it. There's *something*. Something wrong with the way Oxley died, something wrong with the way his Machine didn't self-destruct when he died. Something connecting him and the Hallams. Something's going on."

She smiled. "Copper's intuition?"

"Something like that."

We finished our meals, decided to skip dessert, went straight to coffee. I said, "There was a bit of an atmosphere in the room today."

Sachs was spooning sugar into her cup. "Was there?"

"Yes, Sachs, there was, and you know it."

She stirred her coffee. "Things aren't progressing as well as my superiors would like," she said, setting the spoon down in her saucer. "They're talking about moving you all to a secure facility somewhere."

"That's not going to work," I said.

"No, I told them that. And Regis told *me* that. But they want solid results and everything's been a bit...*fuzzy* so far, so they're thinking about putting you somewhere that will help you concentrate."

"That sounds quite unpleasant," I said.

"It doesn't have to be." She took a sip of coffee. "But it might. Anyway, I gave Regis the bad news this morning, before you turned up."

"Good of everyone to share the tidings with me."

"The group dynamics are your business, not mine."

I sat back and crossed my arms. "It might be advisable," I said, "not to trust Regis too much. Or the others." She started to say something, but I went on, "I know you don't trust us already, and there are good reasons for that. But Regis in particular. Keep a very careful eye on him."

"You think he's planning something?"

"He's *always* planning something."

"That's another thing I don't understand," she said. "Regis saved your life – at least, he gave you a second chance – but you can't stand him."

"He thought I'd be useful to him; that's the only reason he offered me the chance to come back. It's the only reason any of us are here. None of us could have afforded the fee. Pep's his bodyguard, Jan Tyrian's his expert on Machines and nanotechnology. I was supposed to run his computer security. Fuck that."

"Seems... ungrateful."

"I've known him a lot longer than you have," I said. "Trust me, it's not."

"So you ran off and joined the police service."

"So I ran off and joined the police service," I agreed. "I kept my head down, made myself useful. Dammit, Sachs, I *liked* being a police officer. And now that's all over. So if I get a bit grumpy and cynical about all this from time to time, you'll have to forgive me."

She finished her espresso and returned her cup to its saucer. "Know what I think? I think you have a chip on your shoulder. Poor boy rescued by a rich man's charity. You know you couldn't turn him down but you hate him for making the offer."

I'd already spent some time talking to shrinks brought in by Sachs and her team, so this wasn't quite the devastatingly stinging insight she'd probably intended it to be, and I rolled with it. I said, "You're lucky I *am* here. I get the feeling I'm the only one telling you anything useful."

She pursed her lips, then she picked up her phone and checked the time. "We'd better get you back before you turn into a pumpkin," she said, signalling the waiter for the bill.

"It wouldn't be the first time," I said. She gave me a level, calculating look. "Joke," I said. "Or maybe not."

"You want to watch that sense of humour, Frank," she told me. "It'll get you in trouble one day."

In the event, Sachs's threat of a move to some government bunker or other never materialised. Things went on as before, an endless round of meetings and interviews and debriefings and flat-out interrogations. Pep was starting to look bored because she hadn't hurt anyone for a while, Jan Tyrian was starting to look bored because he was basically having to deal with a primitive species and he was tired of having to use baby language to explain things. Regis wasn't starting to look bored. He was in his element, manipulating everybody, pointing them in the right directions in order to get whatever it was he wanted. He looked like a man whose plans were going just the way he wanted them to.

I was bored because... well, everything was boring. The interviewers asked me the same questions and I gave them the same answers, or not depending on what the four of us had agreed we could tell the natives. I sat in the flat reading novels of varying awfulness. I went for walks. Even the walks were getting boring.

"Can we not go somewhere else?" I asked Andrew one day as we walked up the steep path up Parliament Hill. "I have this view memorised already."

This obviously gave him pause. The routine was well-established by now; Andrew and I walked from the flat, through Regent's Park, and up to the top of the hill. Two more minders flanked us at a discreet distance, with a third following, while another waited in one of the SUVs on the road at the bottom of the hill. It was always the same.

"Well, I'll put it to the boss," he said amiably. "See what she says, okay?"

"Fine," I said.

It was a bright, breezy day and the top of Parliament Hill was covered in tourists and kids and picnickers and lovers out for a stroll. It was never this busy in films. We found a space on one of the benches and sat down, and a few moments later a stout middle-aged woman in a worn-looking sun dress and sensible shoes sat down beside me and made us hutch along to make room. She took out her phone and started to take photos of the quite startling view down into central London.

Myself, I'd had enough of this view quite a while ago. I could draw it from memory; the only value of these outings was to get some fresh air and not sit in a room somewhere for a while. I wondered idly whether this was what my life would look like from now on, shuttling between interrogations and pretty views until I went completely out of my mind.

"You can call me Christine," said the woman beside me.

I turned my head. She wasn't looking at me; she was still photographing the view. "Beg pardon?"

"Christine," she said. "You can call me Christine."

"Okay," I said, bracing myself for a stream-of-consciousness recitation of her gripes with the government, the social services, the NHS, the Secret State, her neighbours, Transport for London, whatever.

Instead, she said, quite calmly, "I'll thank you not to mention us to the Security Services again."

I glanced at Andrew, but he was looking into the distance, hands folded in his lap, smiling a little. He seemed to have forgotten I was there, and I felt an icy finger go up the back of my neck.

"You read Sachs's report, then," I said.

"As you thought we would," she said, lowering her phone. "That was cute, Francesco. Irresponsible, but cute. You couldn't be sure one of us would see that report."

"I thought it was worth a try," I said. I looked around for the other minders, but they were nowhere to be seen.

"Well, it's made some work for us; we'll have to tidy things up. But to be honest it was about time one of us had a little chat with you."

If I'd given the stories any credence at all, I supposed I'd imagined the Elders as a shadowy cabal of ancients, not dumpy middle-aged women in cheap sun dresses sitting on benches on Parliament Hill. I said, "I have some questions of my own."

She turned and looked at me, and there was a serene agelessness to her eyes that was quite scary. She was probably as thoroughly modded as it was possible to be and still look human. "Perhaps it would be best if you just listened, Francesco."

"Yes," I said, chastened. "Yes, perhaps it would."

She looked at the view and I saw her smile faintly. "In pursuit of his own convoluted and no doubt nefarious agenda, Regis has decided to take advantage of a situation on your old beat," she said. "It took us a long time to find the Hallams, and now he's put them to flight it'll take us a long time to find them again, and that's annoying."

"I was already investigating that before he even got involved," I said.

"No you weren't," she told me. "He was working on it long before you came along. If it had just been you the Hallams would have managed to keep a lid on it, but Regis decided it would be an ideal situation to attract the attention of the Security Services."

"He sent the avatar."

"Not the first one. He sent the second one, the one that beat you up. I don't imagine he was terribly worried whether it killed you or not, so long as it provoked a response from Sachs's superiors."

"Did he kill Oxley too?"

She smiled again, but this time it was a sad smile, one touched with regret. "No," she said. "No, good guess but that was something else, completely unconnected. But it was another thing Regis thought he could use, and it's another black mark against his name." I wondered just how angry the Elders were with Regis, what they would do to him. "He thinks he's clever," she went on. "But he's really not."

"I'm just a passenger," I said. "I have no idea what's going on. Regis says someone rewrote the original message and piggybacked themselves here with us."

Christine made a rude noise. "Have you any idea how hard that would be?"

"I do, actually."

She looked at me again, and this time she grinned, just for a moment. She rummaged in her bag for a moment, came up holding a car key on an electronic fob. She held them out to me. "There's a van parked on a meter on Regent's Park Road, near the canal bridge," she said. "Do yourself a favour, Francesco. Get out of here. It'll only bring you grief if you stay." When I just sat looking at the key, she said, "You won't get another chance, I promise you."

I glanced at Andrew, but he was still lost in contemplation of the view. "Why are you giving me these?"

"You're an innocent bystander, Francesco," she said. "Make yourself scarce, start again, keep your head down. We'll deal with this now."

I had the uncomfortable feeling that I was a little boy who had just been dismissed by his headteacher. I said, "I don't appreciate being patted on the head and told to fuck off."

"That's too bad," she said with a grim little smile. "Because it's all you're going to get." She waggled the key in front of my face. "Last chance, Francesco."

I thought about it a moment longer, then I reached out and took the key. "Anything else?"

"We might check in with you, from time to time," she said. "But don't count on it. Now go. I'll stick around for a while and make sure your friend doesn't wake up prematurely."

I stood up and looked at her. There was no point memorising her face because by this time tomorrow she would probably look completely different. I said, "What are the Hallams to you?"

"Unfinished business," she said. She shooed me away. "Go."

I walked down the hill without looking back. On Regent's Park Road, near the canal, I held up the keyfob and started clicking the button, and a moment later I was rewarded with a blink of indicators a little further along the line of parked cars.

The lights belonged to a grubby white Berlingo van, the sort of thing you saw on the roads all the time and never noticed. In the back, covered with a sheet, was a Machine. When I put my hand on its surface, I felt it start to wake up.

I stood at the open back doors of the van, thinking. The Elders had broken into my cellar, stolen my Machine, brought it to London, and waited for an opportunity to present it to me. In itself, that wasn't a particularly complicated operation, if you assumed they knew how to get into the cellar in the first place, but it was a quiet demonstration of what they were capable of. *We can do this kind of thing with our eyes shut. Imagine what we can do when we really put our minds to it.*

I closed the doors, went round and sat in the driver's seat. In the glove compartment, tucked in among dusters and tubes of mints and old parking permits, was a battered wallet. In the wallet were five hundred pounds in twenty pound notes, a couple of credit cards in the name of Duncan Wallace, and a driving licence in the same name. Duncan Wallace lived in Hackney and, judging by the photograph on the licence, he was me, the poor bastard.

There was still time to change my mind, but that option had evaporated as soon as Christine dangled the key to the van in front of me. My life hadn't really belonged to me since sometime before I was despatched to Dronfield Farm, and it was time to change that.

I started the engine, put the van into gear, and drove off.

I got the Machine to compile a simple phone and I called Sachs's number.

"That was a cheap trick, Frank," she said.

Dave Hutchinson

It hadn't been my trick, but there was no need for her to know that. "I would apologise, but I'm all out of sympathy," I said.

"Where are you?"

"Not going to tell you that, sorry."

"Come back in," she said. "It's not too late. We can talk about this."

"It's way too late," I told her. "It was already too late when we first met."

There was a silence at the other end of the line, then Sachs said, "What do you mean?"

"This whole thing is a scam," I said. "It's a con to get Regis into your hands and make you think you're in control of the situation, but you're not at all. What has he told you he wants?"

Another silence. "If you come back, I'll tell you."

"I'm guessing he's been trailing clues in front of you for months, little bits and pieces to get your attention, and when he thought you were good and ready he fed you me and Dronfield Farm. Who told you I was going to meet him in London?"

She took a moment to answer that. "We had a tip-off."

"Yeah, right. We've been *played*, Sachs. He *wanted* you to round us up. He wanted to be in a position to get something from you."

There was another silence, this time a long one. I imagined Sachs emailing or texting on another phone or just writing a note and giving it to someone.

"We can meet somewhere," she said finally, and I heard an edge of anger in her voice. "Venue of your choice, anywhere you like. I'll come alone."

"Oh, please, Sachs. Don't insult my intelligence, it's already been insulted enough. All that stuff about people piggybacking back here on our signal? It's bollocks. The best thing you can do right now is lock Regis and the other two up and throw away the key."

More silence.

I sighed. "They've done a runner, haven't they."

"What's that noise in the background? Is that engines? Are you on a boat?"

"They've all gone and they've taken whatever it was Regis talked you into giving him and by now they've changed their appearance and you'll never see them again, Sachs. I'm all you've got left."

86

"We know you're here now, Frank. We'll find you."

"With respect, you couldn't find your arse with your hands and a pack of hunting dogs." And neither could I, apparently. We'd both been played; Regis needed someone clueless like me to make the whole thing look plausible, and he stampeded me in the right directions and I'd fallen for it.

More silence. This time, I could almost hear the fury at the other end of the line. She said, "Can *you* find them?"

"Maybe," I said. "Eventually."

"I'm authorised to make a deal," she said without hesitation.

"That sounds like quite a boast," I said. "What I think is, you'll make a deal and then clear it with your superiors afterward. I imagine you're in quite a lot of trouble right now, what with losing us *and* whatever Regis got away with."

"You're such a dick, Frank. You're all dicks. Five hundred years of scientific advance and what did you do with it? Destroy the fucking human race."

Jesus, he'd actually gone ahead and told her about the Extinction. I wouldn't have put it past him to spin a tale about a Golden Age with thriving colonies on far-flung exoplanets, but he'd played it straight, and I thought that was significant. He'd been trying to scare her into doing something for him.

I said, "That may not happen now. We've introduced too many changes to the timeline." The difference between me and Sachs was that I might, conceivably, still be around in five hundred years' time to see if this was true or not.

"It doesn't matter," she said. "It *did* happen. You *did* fuck up. And you ran away."

"The Extinction wasn't my fault, Sachs. And you'd have taken the chance too, in my place."

I heard her take a deep breath, getting control of her anger. "Jesus." I thought if we stayed on the phone much longer I would hear Sachs banging her forehead against the nearest flat surface. "What is *wrong* with you people?"

"What did Regis want?"

This time, she thought about it for a long while before answering. "He wanted a file," she said. "And if you want to know any more than that you'll have to hear it from me in person."

It must be a hell of a file, for Regis to come up with such a convoluted and risky scheme to get sight of it. I said, "I told you not to trust him."

"Very good, Frank," she said. "You win. Congratulations."

"It's not about winning, Sachs. I haven't won anything. I have no job and no home and I'm on the run; how is that winning?"

"You're still way ahead of me."

"If I am, it's unusual. Goodbye, Sachs." I hung up and sat looking about the deck of the ferry. I thought about Christine's line about 'tidying up' and wondered how far the Elders would go to cover their tracks. Would Sachs and her colleagues even remember any of this in a couple of weeks' time? With patience and care and the right resources, it should be possible to edit this whole thing out of personal and institutional memory. I wondered if that had been Regis's intention all along, to get his hands on the file and then manoeuvre the Elders into covering his tracks for him, in which case all I'd done was help. I supposed it was possible that the 'tidying up' would include me, that one day I'd wake up with a new name and a new face and a new life and no memory at all of what I'd been doing for the past few months, but I suspected the Elders would want to deal with Regis, and it would be handy to leave me alone to try and track him down. We were going to have a difference of opinion about what to do when I finally did catch up with him, but we could cross that bridge when we came to it.

I got up and went over to the railing and unobtrusively dropped the phone into Belfast Lough. Then I turned and headed for the car deck. We'd be docking soon.

About the Author

Dave Hutchinson is a science fiction writer who was born in Sheffield in 1960 and read American Studies at the University of Nottingham. He subsequently moved into journalism, writing for *The Weekly News* and the *Dundee Courier* for almost 25 years. He is best known for his Fractured Europe series (Solaris), which has received multiple award nominations, with the third novel, *Europe in Winter*, winning the BSFA Award for Best Novel. His novella *The Push* (NewCon Press), a tale involving the birth of faster-than-light travel and speculating on the consequences of settling other worlds, was shortlisted for the 2010 BSFA award for short fiction. Hutchinson has also edited two anthologies and co-edited a third. His short story "The Incredible Exploding Man", which featured in the first *Solaris Rising* anthology, was selected for Gardner Dozois' 29th *Year's Best* anthology.

NewCon Press Novellas Set 5: The Alien Among Us

Nomads – Dave Hutchinson

Are there really refugees from another time living among us?
And, if so, what dreadful event are they fleeing from? When a
high speed car chase leads Police Sergeant Frank Grant to
Dronfield Farm, he finds himself the focus of unwanted attention
from Internal Affairs and is confronted by questions he's not sure
he ever wants to hear answered.

Morpho – Philip Palmer

When the corpse on the mortuary slab sits up and speaks to
Hayley, asking for her help, she thinks she's losing her mind. If
only it were that simple... Philip Palmer delivers a tense fast-
paced tale of a secret society that governs our world from the
shadows, of immortality at a terrible price and events that lead to
the overthrow of social order.

The Man Who Would Be Kling – Adam Roberts

When two people ask the manager at Kabul Station to take them
into the Afghanizone he refuses. What sane person wouldn't?
Said to represent alien visitation, the zone is deadly. Nothing
works there. Electrical items malfunction or simply blow up. The
pair go in anyway, and the biggest surprise is when one of them
walks out again. Nobody survives the zone, so how has she?

Macsen Against the Jugger – Simon Morden

Two centuries after the Earth fell to alien machines known as the
Visitors, humanity survives in sparse nomadic tribes. Macsen is an
adventurer, undertaking hazardous quests to please Hona Loy.
Macsen never fails, but this time he is pitted against a deadly
Jugger. Can he somehow survive, or will it fall to his faithful
companion Laylaw to tell the tale of his noble death?

NewCon Press Novellas

Released in sets of four, each novella is an independent stand-alone story. Each set is linked by shared cover art, split between the books, providing separate covers that link to form a single image greater than the parts.

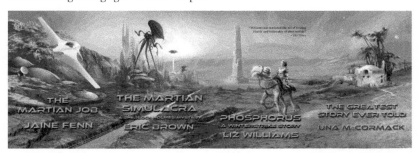

Set 1: Science Fiction
Novellas by Alastair Reynolds, Simon Morden, Anne Charnock, Neil Williamson.
Cover art by Chris Moore

Set 2: Dark Thrillers
Novellas by Simon Clark, Alison Littlewood, Sarah Lotz, Jay Caselberg.
Cover art by Vincent Sammy

Set 3: The Martian Quartet
Novellas by Jaine Fenn, Eric Brown, Liz Williams, Una McCormack.
Cover art by Jim Burns

Set 4: Strange Tales
Novellas by Gary Gibson, Adam Roberts, Ricardo Pinto, Hal Duncan.
Cover art by Ben Baldwin

Set 5: The Alien Among Us
Novellas by Dave Hutchinson, Philip Palmer, Adam Roberts, Simon Morden.
Cover art by Peter Hollinghurst

 Each novella is available separately in paperback or as a limited numbered hardback edition, signed by the author. Each set is available as a strictly limited lettered slipcase set, containing all four of the books as signed dust-jacketed hardbacks and featuring the combined artwork as a wrap-around.

www.newconpress.co.uk

Immanion Press

Purveyors of Speculative Fiction
www.immanion-press.com

Vivia by Tanith Lee

Tanith Lee was writing grimdark fantasy even before it was known as a genre. Gritty, savage and darkly erotic, *Vivia* is one of the author's darkest - and finest - works. Vivia, the neglected daughter of a vicious warlord, discovers strange, lightless caverns deep beneath her father's castle. Here she finds an entity she believes is a living god and, in her loneliness, seeks its favour. After war and disease devastate her father's lands, Vivia is taken captive by the hedonistic Prince Zulgaris and kept as his concubine. In this barbaric land, where life means very little, and the spectre of the plague haunts the alleys and markets of even the greatest city, circumstances can change very quickly. No life is safe, and treachery abounds. Perhaps, in such a brutal world, only remote pitiless creatures like Vivia can survive unscathed. But at what cost? ISBN: 978-1-907737-98-5 £12.99 $16.99

Songs to Earth and Sky edited by Storm Constantine

Six writers explore the eight seasonal festivals of the year, dreaming up new beliefs and customs, new myths, new dehara – the gods of Wraeththu. As different communities develop among Wraeththu, the androgynous race who have inherited a ravaged earth, so fresh legends spring up – or else ghosts from the inception of their kind come back to haunt them. From the silent, snow-heavy forests of Megalithican mountains, through the lush summer fields of Alba Sulh, into the hot, shimmering continent of Olathe, this book explores the Wheel of the Year, bringing its powerful spirits and landscapes to vivid life. Nine brand new tales, including a novella, a novelette and a short story from Storm herself, and stories from *Wendy Darling, Nerine Dorman, Suzanne Gabriel, Fiona Lane* and *E. S. Wynn.* ISBN 978-1-907737-84-8 £11.99 $15.50 pbk

Lightning Source UK Ltd.
Milton Keynes UK
UKHW012020120319
338988UK00001B/397/P